Love Written In The Waves

Two hearts. One cruise.
A destiny written in the waves.

By
Jessica Phipps

Copyright © 2026 Jessica Phipps.

All Rights Reserved.

ISBN
Paperback: 979-8-90321-056-5
Hardback: 979-8-90321-057-2

Table of Contents

Dedication

To my son, **Tucker** — the one who looked at me one day and said, *"You read enough books… why not write one of your own?"*

Those simple words lit a spark in me, and this story exists because you believed I could create one of my own. Thank you for inspiring me, encouraging me, and reminding me that dreams don't have deadlines.

To the rest of my family — thank you for always being there when I need you the most. Your love, support, and steady presence have carried me through every chapter of my life.

Chapter One

The champagne was vintage, the suite was sprawling, and the second pillow was a mocking reminder of the man currently honeymooning with his paralegal in Cabo.

I stood on the private teak veranda of the Star of the Seas, my white silk wrap fluttering in the humid breeze as the Miami skyline began its slow retreat. I should have been devastated. Instead, I felt a dangerous, buzzing clarity. I kept the booking, the offshore excursions, and the five-thousand-dollar wardrobe. The only thing I discarded was two hundred pounds of lying fiancé. "To me," I whispered, raising my crystal flute to the Atlantic.

"A waste of good bubbles to drink alone."

The voice was a low, melodic rumble that seemed to vibrate through the glass partition separating each balcony from the next.

I stiffened, turning my head just enough to see him. He was leaning against the railing of the adjacent suite, a silhouette of hard angles and effortless grace. He wasn't wearing a suit; he wore a charcoal linen shirt with the sleeves rolled up to reveal forearms corded with muscle and dusted with dark hair. In the golden light of the sunset, his skin looked like polished bronze.

He was the most beautiful man she had ever seen, staring at her with the shameless intensity of a predator who had just spotted something shimmering in the grass.

"It's a big ship," I said, my voice steadier than my heartbeat. "I'm sure I can find someone to toast with if I get lonely."

The stranger took a slow sip of what looked like neat bourbon, his dark eyes never leaving hers. "Loneliness is a choice on a voyage like this, but a woman in a wedding-white robe drinking prestige cuvée at departure? That's a story."

He moved closer to the partition, the scent of sandalwood and expensive sea salt drifting over to her. Up close, his eyes weren't just dark—they were the color of the deep Bahamian trenches they were currently sailing toward.

"I'm Julian," he said, his mouth curving into a smirk that promised absolutely no good intentions. "And if you're looking for a New Beginning, I find the best ones usually start with a bit of trouble." I'm Elena, nice to meet you, Julian. I felt a flush creep up my neck that had nothing to do with the heat. I looked at his hand—large, tan, and notably ringless.

"I'm not looking for trouble, Julian."

"Liars are my favorite kind of passengers," he murmured, his gaze dropping to her lips. "Welcome aboard, Elena. Try not to drown before we hit the Bahamas."

A laugh escaped me before I could stop it, short, disbelieving, edged with something reckless. "I'll do my best," I said, lifting a glass in a mock salute. "I hear drowning is terrible for the hair."

Julian's smile deepened, slow and devastating. "Good. I'd hate to see a woman like you go to waste."

The ship's horn bellowed, vibrating through the metal beneath my bare feet. The deck shuddered as the *Star of the Seas* pushed fully away from the port, the last sliver of Miami shrinking into a glittering line on the horizon. The breeze picked up, warm and salted, tugging at the wrap and sending a shiver across my skin.

Julian noticed. Of course he did.

"You cold?" he asked, voice dipping into something that felt like concern wrapped in temptation.

"I'm fine," I said too quickly.

His eyes flicked over me, not lewd, but observant, like he was cataloging details he had no business noticing. "You don't look fine."

"And you don't look like someone who minds his own business."

He chuckled, low and rich. "Touche."

For a moment, neither of us spoke. The ocean stretched endlessly ahead, a darkening expanse that felt like possibility and danger all at once. I took another sip of champagne, letting the bubbles burn pleasantly down my throat.

"So," Julian said, leaning his forearms on the railing, "are you going to tell me why you're drinking alone in a honeymoon suite?"

I stiffened. "Who says it's a honeymoon suite?"

He arched a brow. "The champagne. The robe. The look in your eyes is like you're trying very hard not to think about something or someone."

I swallowed hard. "You're very observant."

"I'm very bored," he corrected. "And you're interesting."

The word hit me harder than it should have. Interesting. Not pitied. Not fragile. Not abandoned.

I turned fully toward him, letting the robe fall open just enough to show the neckline of the silk slip beneath. His gaze flicked down, then back up, slower this time.

"My fiancé," I said, tasting the bitterness of the word, "is in Cabo. With his paralegal."

Julian's expression didn't shift into sympathy. It turned into something far more dangerous, to amusement. "Ah. So, you're celebrating your freedom."

"Something like that."

"Good," he said. "He sounds like an idiot."

I blinked. "You don't even know him."

"I don't need to," Julian replied. "Any man who lets you out of his sight long enough to end up on a balcony next to me is an idiot."

Heat pooled low in my stomach, unwelcome, unexpected, undeniable.

"You're very confident," I said.

He shrugged one shoulder. "I'm honest."

"And what exactly are you being honest about right now?"

"That I'm trying very hard not to climb over this railing," he said, voice dropping to a velvet murmur, "and kiss the look off your face."

My breath caught.

The ship rocked gently, the ocean humming beneath us like a living thing. The air between us tightened, stretched, pulled taut like a thread ready to snap. I should have stepped back. I should have remembered that I was newly single, newly humiliated, newly free.

Instead, I whispered, "What look?"

Julian's eyes darkened, the sunset catching in them like embers. "The one that says you're done being careful."

My pulse thundered in my ears.

He straightened, finishing the last of his bourbon in one smooth swallow.

"Goodnight, Elena," he said, voice rougher now. "Try not to drink all the champagne without me."

Before I could respond, he disappeared into his suite, sliding the glass door shut behind him.

I stood frozen, champagne glass trembling slightly in my hand, the ocean wind whipping around me.

Done being careful.

Maybe I was.

Maybe for once in my life, I wanted to see what happened when I stopped choosing the safe things.

When I finally stepped back inside, the second pillow on the bed didn't feel mocking.

It felt like an invitation.

Chapter Two
Two Months Earlier

Everything felt wild. Three weeks until the wedding, and every day seemed to move faster than the last. Todd stood beside the towering display of cakes, the soft glow of the bakery lights catching the excitement in his eyes. The moment the owner brought out the platter of samples, we both leaned in like kids about to open presents. I reached for the white cake with strawberry and cream filling first. It was soft, sweet, and perfect. Todd tasted it too, and the way his eyes lit up told me everything. We didn't even need to discuss it — that was our cake.

Moments like that made everything feel right.

Easy.

Like we were exactly who we were supposed to be.

But they were rare.

As we stepped out of the bakery, Todd pulled me close. His arms wrapped around me, warm and sure, and when he kissed me, the rest of the world blurred out. I felt that familiar rush in my chest, that dizzy, overwhelming thought: *I am so in love with this man. I can't wait to spend forever with him.*

By the time we got home, the air between us was already charged. We barely made it through the door before we were on each other, laughing breathlessly as our lips met again. His hands slid to my waist, tugging me closer, and I felt my pulse jump.

We stumbled down the hallway, still tangled in each other and kissing as though we'd been apart for weeks instead of hours Todd's fingers brushed my skin as he lifted my shirt, and the warmth of his touch sent a shiver through me. I pulled his shirt over his head, my hands roaming instinctively, drawn to him like gravity. When we reached the bedroom, he guided me back onto the bed with a mix of urgency and tenderness that left me breathless. The look in his eyes — hungry, loving, completely focused on me — made my heart race. He leaned in, his lips brushing my skin, slow and deliberate, each kiss sending sparks through me. My hands curled into the sheets as he moved closer, his breath warm against my thigh, then he moved over and started kissing my pussy lips. He slid his tongue into my wet pussy and started to lick and suck on my clit. It felt so amazing, my back arched as he teased me with his tongue as he slid his fingers deep in my opening, and I let out a low moan. I was about to reach my climax when he stopped. He took his pants off and entered his big, hard cock into my pussy, I love the way his hard dick felt deep inside me. He started thrusting faster and faster as he was kissing my lips, and I moaned in his mouth. We were both getting close to climax as he thrusted his dick harder into my pussy until we both hit our climax at the same time. I could feel my pussy contracting against his hard cock as he released all his cum inside me. He rolled off of me, and we held each other and fell asleep in each other's arms.

But the next morning, reality returned like a cold draft under the door.

Todd was already up, already dressed, already checking his phone.

"I've got to run in," he said, not looking up.

"Just for a few hours."

A few hours turned into the whole day.

And that became the pattern.

Two weeks until the wedding

I sat alone at the venue appointment, staring at swatches of linen napkins while the coordinator asked questions I didn't know how to answer without him.

"Will your fiancé be joining us?" she asked gently.

"He…got caught up at the office," I said, forcing a smile. "He's been really busy."

Busy. Always busy.

He missed the florist appointment. The menu tasting. The meeting with the DJ. He promised he'd make the final walkthrough, but even that ended with a text:

I'm so sorry, babe. Emergency at work. I'll make it up to you.

I wanted to believe him. I always did. But every time I sat alone at another appointment, every time I watched other couples laughing together, choosing things together, planning a life together…something inside me tightened.

One week until the wedding

I found myself sitting in the bridal boutique, surrounded by mirrors and lace and soft lighting. My dress is hanging on the rack beside me, shimmering like a promise.

Todd was supposed to be there for the final fitting.

He wasn't

My phone buzzed.

Running late. Don't wait on me.

I stared at the message, my throat tightening. The seamstress smiled kindly, unaware of the storm inside me.

"Ready to try it on?" she asked.

I nodded, even though I suddenly felt like I couldn't breathe.

As she zipped me into the gown, I stared at my reflection. The dress was beautiful, everything I had dreamed of. But the woman wearing it looked unsure.

Lonely.

Like she was marrying a man who was slipping through her fingers one missed appointment at a time.

That night, Todd finally came home after ten. He kissed my forehead, told me he loved me, told me work was insane, and told me he couldn't wait to marry me.

And I believed him. Or I tried too.

But as I lay awake beside him, staring at the ceiling, a quiet thought crept in, one I didn't want to acknowledge.

If he can't show up now…when will he?

Chapter Three
Two Weeks Later

Life can change in the blink of an eye. I never imagined that after months of planning our wedding—after choosing flowers, tasting cakes, picking out colors and venues—I would discover that my soon-to-be husband had been lying to me all along.

Todd was a high-powered attorney at a major law firm. Long hours were normal for him, or so I thought. I believed he was buried in case files, fighting for clients, doing what he always did. But he wasn't working late on cases. He was working on his paralegal, Jalisa.

He had been having an affair with her the entire time I was planning our wedding.

And the worst part? Looking back, the signs were there. They were everywhere.

Three months before the wedding, we were supposed to meet with the florist to finalize the arrangements. I sat alone at the little round table, surrounded by vases of roses and peonies, pretending I wasn't embarrassed when the florist asked, "Will your fiancé be joining us?"

"He got stuck at the office," I said, forcing a smile. "He's really swamped."

It became my script. My excuse. My shield.

Two months before the wedding, we had our final walk-through. I walked the entire property alone, the ceremony, space, reception hall, and bridal suite, while the coordinator kept glancing at the door, expecting Todd to appear at any moment.

"He wanted to be here," I lied. "Something urgent came up."

One month before the wedding, we were supposed to pick out our first-dance song together. I sat on the couch with my laptop open, listening to romantic ballads by myself while Todd texted me:

Still at work. Don't wait for me, pick what you want."

I told myself it was temporary. That he was stressed. That he was doing all of this for us.

But now I knew the truth.

He wasn't working late. He wasn't stressed. He wasn't building a future with me.

He was building one with her.

Two days ago, while he was in the shower, his phone rang. The name *Jalisa* flashed across the screen. I answered, assuming it was something work-related. But the moment I said hello, her voice came through the line—soft, familiar, intimate.

"Hey, babe."

My stomach dropped. Heat rushed to my face. "Why the hell are you calling my fiancé, *babe*?" I snapped.

She hung up instantly.

When Todd stepped out of the shower, towel around his waist, I was shaking with anger and disbelief.

"Why did Jalisa just call your phone?" I demanded, "And why is she calling you *babe*?"

He froze. For a long moment, he said nothing. Then, with a heavy breath, he finally spoke.

"Because… I've been sleeping with her. She's fallen in love with me. But I'm not in love with her. It was just sex for me; I only love you."

His words hit me like a punch. Tears spilled down my cheeks before I could stop them.

"Didn't I give you enough sex? And how can you say you love me," I choked out, "when you're cheating on me with another woman while I was planning our wedding?"

He rushed to defend himself. "She means nothing to me. It just happened one night and… we couldn't stop. It's been going on for four months."

Four months. The entire time we'd been planning our future.

I sat on the edge of the bed, burying my face in my hands as sobs shook through me. When he tried to come closer, to comfort me—as if that were even possible—I jumped up and backed away.

"How could you?" I shouted. "After everything we've done, everything we've paid for, everything we planned?"

I ripped the engagement ring off my finger, opened the door, and hurled it at him. It hit the floor with a sharp, final clink.

"We're done," I said, my voice breaking. "I never want to see you again."

I walked out, got in my car, and drove to the nearest motel. The shock clung to me like a second skin. I couldn't understand how someone I loved so deeply could betray me so cruelly and still expect me to walk down the aisle.

I booked a room for three weeks—just enough time to find a house and figure out what my new life as a single woman would look like.

The first night, I cried until my throat was burning. The second night, I stared at the ceiling, numb and hollow. The third night, something inside me hardened.

And I thought we had already paid for our honeymoon cruise.

And in that moment, something inside me shifted.

I decided I was going on that cruise—alone. Not to escape, but to begin again. To breathe. To heal. To start my new beginning on my own terms.

For the first time in months, years, I felt a spark of something I thought I'd lost.

Hope.

The morning after I decided to take the cruise, I woke up in the motel with a clarity I hadn't in months. The cheap curtains glowed with early sunlight, and for the first time since the breakup, I didn't feel crushed under the weight of what Todd had done.

I felt…free.

I drove back to the apartment while he was at work, letting myself in with my key that I never returned. The place looked the same, neat, modern, cold. A life we had built together, but one that suddenly felt like it belonged to strangers. I pulled out my suitcases and began packing.

Not the wedding dress. Not the lingerie I'd bought for the honeymoon. Not the matching "Mr. & Mrs." passport holders.

Just me. My clothes, my perfume, and makeup.

All my books, a swimsuit I'd bought months ago but never had the confidence to wear.

As I was folding my sundresses into the suitcase, my phone buzzed. Todd.

I stared at the screen, my pulse quickening. For a moment, I considered ignoring it. But something inside me wanted closure.

I answered.

"Elena," he breathed, sounding frantic.

"Please. Can we talk?"

"There's nothing left to talk about."

"Yes, there is," he insisted. "I made a mistake. A horrible one. But we can fix this. We can go to counseling. We can…"

"No," I said firmly. "You don't get to cheat on me for four months and then ask me to fix it with you."

He went quiet. I could hear him breathing, shaky and uneven.

"I love you," he whispered.

I closed my eyes. "You loved the idea of me. The version of me who didn't question your late nights. The version who planned our wedding alone. The version who trusted you."

"Elena.."

"I'm done, Todd."

I hung up before he could say another word.

And just like that, the last thread snapped.

Chapter Four

The heavy, suffocating weight of "Elena and Todd" had officially been incinerated.

Over the last few days, I'd moved through the stages of grief like a woman on a mission. The florist had been canceled. The caterer had been told to keep the deposit for their trouble. The only thing I hadn't touched—the one thing I refused to let him ruin—was the honeymoon.

But I wasn't just coming back to my old life when the ship docked. Before I'd even packed my first suitcase, I'd signed the papers on a gorgeous little beach house tucked away on the coast. It was exactly what I'd always dreamed of: a cedar-shingled sanctuary with a wrap-around porch where the rhythm of the crashing waves would be the only heartbeat I had to answer to. It was just big enough for a single woman, a stack of books, and a very large wine rack.

The hurt Todd had inflicted—the jagged, raw betrayal of finding out about him and his paralegal—had finally hardened into something much more useful: pure, unadulterated fury. And beneath that fury was a shimmering sense of freedom. I was better off. I was *so* much better off.

"Goodbye, Todd," I muttered, slamming my suitcase shut. "And hello, me."

The day of the cruise arrived faster than I expected. I drove to the port with my windows down, letting the warm Miami air whip through my hair. The closer I got, the more the ship came into view, massive, gleaming, impossibly beautiful.

The Star of the Seas.

Our honeymoon ship

My ship now!

I parked, grabbed my luggage, and walked toward the terminal. People bustled around me, families, couples, groups of friends, all buzzing with excitement. For a moment, I felt a ping of loneliness. But then I reminded myself: I wasn't here to mourn what I'd lost. I was here to rediscover who I was.

As I stepped onto the gangway, the ocean breeze hit me full in the face, warm, salty, alive. The ship's horn sounded, deep and resonant, vibrating through my chest.

I inhaled deeply.

This was the beginning.

A crew member handed me a welcome drink, and I took a sip, letting the sweetness settle on my tongue. I walked to the railing, staring out at the endless blue stretching toward the horizon.

And then I did something I didn't expect. I reached into my purse and pulled out the small velvet ring box. I had grabbed it from the apartment without thinking, unsure why I took it.

Now I knew.

I opened the box. The engagement ring was placed back in the box after I threw it at Todd that night. It sparkled in the sunlight, beautiful, expensive, and meaningless.

My heart thumped.

I closed the box, held it over the railing, and threw it as hard as I could, and I watched it fly high in the air until it finally splashed into the waves.

A weight lifted from my chest so suddenly I gasped.

I wasn't the woman who had been cheated on. I wasn't the woman who had been left behind. I wasn't the woman who had planned a wedding alone.

I was the woman who chose herself. The woman who boarded a ship alone. The woman who was ready for something new.

I then went to find my room to put my luggage away. I opened the balcony door and stepped out into the warmth of Florida.

Standing on the balcony of the *Star of the Seas* now, watching the Florida coastline vanish, Julian's presence at the balcony railing felt like the universe's way of rewarding my bravery. He was the "trouble" I had spent a lifetime avoiding, but as I looked at the way his linen shirt clung to his shoulders, I realized I was done playing it safe.

"You're doing it again," Julian said, his voice dropping an octave as he moved closer to the divider.

"Doing what?" I asked, finally turning my full body toward him, letting the silk robe slip just a fraction of an inch lower on my shoulder.

"Thinking," he said, his dark eyes tracing the line of my collarbone. "You look like a woman who just burned a bridge and is enjoying the warmth of the fire."

I took a long, slow sip of my champagne, meeting his gaze with a boldness that surprised me. "I didn't just burn it, Julian. I blew it up. And I'm moving into a house by the ocean where the only thing I have to worry about is the tide."

Julian's smirk widened, revealing a glimpse of white teeth. He looked like he wanted to reach across the railing and see if my skin felt as soft as it looked. "A beach house. Solitude. It sounds... peaceful." He paused, his gaze darkening with a sudden, sharp intensity. "But peaceful is boring for a woman with fire in her eyes. You've got seven days until we reach the islands. Seven days to be whoever you want to be before you start that quiet life."

He set his bourbon glass down on the teak table and leaned over the partition, his face only inches from mine. I could smell the heat of him, a heady mix of spice and adrenaline.

"Tell me, Elena," he whispered, his breath ghosting over my lips. "In this new life of yours, are you still the girl who plays by the rules? Or are you the girl who finally finds out why they call this the *Star of the Seas*?"

The ship took a deep, rhythmic plunge into a swell, and for a second, I lost my balance. Julian's hand shot out, his fingers wrapping around my forearm to steady me. His grip was firm, his palm searingly hot against my skin. The spark that jumped between us was electric, a physical jolt that made my toes curl into the deck.

I didn't pull away. Instead, I leaned into his touch. "I think the girl who played by the rules stayed on the dock."

Julian's thumb stroked the sensitive skin of my inner wrist; his eyes fixed on mine. "Good," he rasped. "Because I have a feeling the Bahamas has never seen anything quite like what you're about to become."

Chapter Five

I woke to sunlight—real, golden, unapologetic sunlight—pouring through the balcony doors like it owned the place. For a moment, I forgot where I was. The sheets were too soft, the air too warm, the distant hum of the ship too steady to be anything but a dream.

Then the events of last night flickered back like a match being struck.

Julian's hand on my wrist. His breath brushes my lips. That look in his eyes—danger wrapped in charm, heat wrapped in a smile.

I exhaled slowly, letting the memory settle over me like a second skin. I hadn't kissed him. I hadn't crossed any lines. But the *possibility* had been enough to keep my heart racing long after I'd closed my balcony door.

A knock sounded—three slow taps, confident, unhurried.

I froze.

No one knew me on this ship. No one except—

I tightened the belt of my robe and opened the door just enough to see him leaning against the frame, hands in his pockets, sunglasses pushed into his hair. Julian looked like he'd stepped out of a travel magazine and directly onto my welcome mat. "Morning, Elena," he said, his voice still rough with sleep. "Thought I'd check on you. Make sure the girl who doesn't play by the rules survives the night."

My pulse fluttered. "I survived."

"Good." His gaze dipped briefly to the hollow of my throat before returning to my eyes. "Because I have a proposition.

Of course he did.

I crossed my arms, partly to look unimpressed, partly because the robe suddenly felt too thin. "What kind of proposition?

He held up a keycard—sleek, black, embossed with the ship's crest.

"A private tour," he said. "Restricted decks. Hidden lounges. The parts of the ship most passengers never see."

"And why," I asked, arching a brow, "would you offer that to me?"

Julian stepped closer, the corridor lights catching the faint stubble along his jaw. "Because you looked at the ocean last night like a woman who's ready to rewrite her entire story. And I want front-row seats."

My breath caught—not because of the words, but because of the certainty behind them. He wasn't guessing. He wasn't flirting for sport. He *saw* me.

And for the first time in months, years, I felt seen.

I opened the door wider.

"Give me ten minutes," I said.

Julian's smile was slow, wicked, and entirely too confident. "Take five."

He turned and walked down the hall, leaving the faint scent of cedar and heat in his wake.

I closed the door, leaned back against it, and let out a breath I didn't realize I'd been holding.

This was not the honeymoon I'd planned.

It was better.

Julian didn't knock again. He didn't need to. His presence lingered in the hallway long after he walked away, like the echo of a dare I hadn't decided whether to take.

I dressed quickly in a white sundress, loose waves in my hair, and a touch of lip gloss. Nothing dramatic, but enough to make me feel like a woman who was stepping into a new version of herself. A version that didn't apologize for wanting things.

When I opened the door, Julian was leaning against the railing across the hall, arms crossed, sunglasses on, looking like he'd been waiting for me his entire life.

"You took seven minutes," he said, pushing off the rail. "I said five."

"You'll survive," I replied, brushing past him.

He fell into step beside me, his shoulder close enough to graze mine but never quite touching. It was maddening. He was maddening. Every step felt like a silent negotiation—how close he could get without crossing a line, how far I could lean without losing my balance.

"You look different this morning," he said as we reached the elevator.

"Different how?"

"Like you slept with the door open and let the ocean rewrite you."

I rolled my eyes, but my pulse betrayed me. "You're very poetic for someone who drinks bourbon before noon."

He grinned. "Only when the company inspires it."

The elevator doors slid open. He stepped inside first, holding the door with one hand, waiting for me. When I walked in, he moved behind me—close enough that I could feel the warmth of him at my back—not touching. Just… there.

The doors closed.

The air shifted.

Julian lowered his voice. "Tell me something, Elena."

I swallowed. "What?"

"Are you running toward something on this cruise… or away from something?"

I turned to face him, lifting my chin. "Maybe both."

His eyes flicked to my mouth, then back to my eyes. "That's dangerous."

"Why?"

"Because people who are running," he murmured, "are the ones who do the most unpredictable things." The elevator chimed. The doors opened. I stepped out first, needing the space, needing air. Julian followed, slower, like he was giving me a head start.

"Relax," he said, catching up. "I'm not here to push you."

"No?" I challenged.

"No." He paused, then added, "But I'm also not here to pretend I don't want you."

My breath hitched.

There it was—the truth, laid bare between us.

"But wanting you," he continued, "and rushing you are two very different things."

I stopped walking. He stopped, too.

"Julian," I said softly, "I don't know what I want yet."

He stepped closer, but not close enough to touch. Close enough to feel.

"That's the best part," he said. "You don't have to know. You just have to let yourself feel."

The ship rocked gently beneath us, the ocean stretching endlessly ahead. For the first time in months, I felt something other than heartbreak or anger.I felt possibility.

And Julian—dangerous, intoxicating Julian—felt like the spark that could either light my way forward… or burn me alive.

Chapter Six

Julian led me down a quiet corridor marked *Crew Only*, glancing over his shoulder with a grin that said he enjoyed breaking rules far too much. The ship hummed beneath us, a low vibration that made everything feel alive.

"You sure we're allowed back here?" I asked, even though I didn't slow down.

"No," he said simply. "But you look like a woman who's tired of asking permission."

A shiver ran through me—part thrill, part warning. Todd had always insisted on rules. Schedules. Plans. Everything is neat and controlled. And I had followed, thinking that was what love looked like.

But Julian... Julian was the opposite of controlled.

He stopped at a metal door and swiped the black keycard. The lock clicked.

"After you," he murmured.

The room beyond was dim, lit only by soft blue floor lights. It was some kind of observation deck—glass walls curving around the bow of the ship, giving a panoramic view of the endless ocean. Empty. Quiet. Hidden.

My breath caught. "This is beautiful."

Julian stepped in behind me, his voice low. "I thought you'd like it."

I walked toward the glass, placing my palm against the cool surface. The sea stretched out forever, dark and glittering. For a moment, I felt small—but in a way that made me feel free, not trapped.

Julian came to stand beside me, close enough that his sleeve brushed mine. "You're thinking again."

"Maybe."

"About him?"

I stiffened. "No."

He didn't push. He didn't smirk. He just waited.

The truth slipped out before I could stop it. "I keep wondering how I didn't see it. How I let myself believe everything he said."

Julian's jaw tightened. "People like Todd are good at hiding their rot. They count on you being loyal. Trusting. Kind."

I swallowed hard. "I was all of those things."

"And he didn't deserve any of it." The words hit deeper than I expected. I turned to him, and he was already watching me—really watching me. Not with pity. With something sharper. Protective. Admiring.

Dangerous.

"You know," he said softly, "you don't have to pretend you're fine with me."

"I'm not pretending."

"Good." His voice dropped. "Because I don't want the version of you who pretends. I want the version who walked out on a man who didn't value her. The version who threw a ring at his feet and didn't look back."

Heat pooled low in my stomach. "You don't even know me."

Julian stepped closer, slow enough that I could stop him if I wanted to. I didn't.

"I know enough," he murmured. "I know you're brave. I know you're angry. I know you're trying to remember who you were before someone convinced you to shrink."

My breath hitched. "And who do you think I was?"

His fingers brushed my wrist—light, deliberate, sending sparks up my arm. "A woman who didn't apologize for wanting things."

The air thickened between us.

I should have stepped back. I should have said something clever. Instead, I whispered, "And what do you think I want?"

Julian's eyes darkened, but he didn't touch me again. He didn't crowd me. He just let the question hang there, pulsing like a heartbeat.

"That," he said, "is what I want you to figure out."

The ship dipped gently, and I swayed. Julian's hand shot out, steadying me—warm, firm, lingering just a second too long.

My pulse stuttered.

Todd had never touched me like that. Not with intention. Not with awareness. Not like he was memorizing the shape of me.

I stepped back—not because I wanted distance, but because I needed air.

Julian let me go, but his gaze stayed locked on mine. "Elena," he said quietly, "you don't owe me anything. Not a kiss. Not a confession. Not a damn thing."

"Then why bring me here?"

His smile was slow, wicked, and somehow gentle. "Because you deserve to feel something good again. Something that's yours. Not his."

The words hit harder than any flirtation.

I turned back to the glass, watching the waves crash against the bow. My reflection stared back at me—hair tousled, cheeks flushed, eyes bright with something I hadn't seen in a long time.

Possibility.

Julian came to stand beside me again, close but not touching. "Seven days," he murmured. "Seven days to decide who you want to be."

I exhaled, the tension between us humming like electricity.

"Then I guess," I said softly, "I should make them count."

Julian's grin was pure trouble. "That's the spirit."

Chapter Seven

The dining room glittered like a jewelry box—crystal chandeliers, polished marble floors, and tables draped in white linen that shimmered under candlelight. I hadn't expected the *Star of the Seas* to feel this grand, but tonight it looked like a palace floating across the water.

Julian was waiting for me at the entrance.

He wore a charcoal suit that fit him like it had been tailored by someone who understood the architecture of his shoulders. When he saw me, he didn't smile right away. His gaze swept over me—slow, deliberate, appreciative—before settling on my eyes.

"Elena," he said, offering his arm. "You're going to ruin every man's appetite in this room."

I slipped my hand into the crook of his elbow, feeling the warmth of him through the fabric. "Good thing I'm only interested in ruining yours."

His low laugh vibrated through me.

We were led to a table near the balcony windows, the ocean stretching out in a dark, endless ribbon beyond the glass. The waiter poured champagne, and Julian lifted his glass toward mine.

"To new beginnings," he said.

I hesitated for a heartbeat—Todd's ghost flickering at the edge of my thoughts. The last time I'd toasted to anything, it had been to a future that didn't exist.

But Julian held my gaze, steady, and patient.

I clinked my glass against his. "To new beginnings."

Dinner was a blur of laughter, teasing, and the kind of conversation that made time slip through my fingers. Julian was infuriatingly charming—quick-witted, observant, and just dangerous enough to make my pulse skip.

But now and then, a shadow crept in.

A memory of Todd's lies. The sting of betrayal. The fear of trusting someone again.Julian noticed each time.

He didn't pry. He didn't push. He simply shifted the conversation or brushed his fingers lightly against mine, grounding me in the present.

By the time dessert arrived, the band in the corner had begun to play—a slow, velvety melody that wrapped around the room like warm silk.

Julian stood and extended his hand. "Dance with me."

I stared at his hand for a moment, my heart thudding. Todd had hated dancing. He'd always said he felt awkward, that it wasn't his thing. I'd stopped asking years ago.

But Julian… Julian looked like a man who knew exactly what to do with a dance floor.

I placed my hand in his.

He led me to the center of the room, one hand settling at the small of my back, the other holding mine gently but firmly. The moment he pulled me close, the world softened around the edges.

"You're tense," he murmured.

"I'm fine."

"You're lying."

I exhaled shakily. "Maybe a little."

His thumb brushed the back of my hand. "Then let me help."

He guided me into the rhythm—slow, swaying, intimate. My body relaxed against his, my cheek brushing his jaw as we moved. The scent of him—warm, clean, a hint of spice—wrapped around me.

For the first time in a long time, I felt wanted. Not for convenience. Not for appearance. But for me.

Julian lowered his head slightly, his lips near my ear. "You're thinking again."

"Maybe."

"Stop."

"How?"

He pulled back just enough to look at me. His eyes were dark, intent, searching.

"Like this," he whispered.

And then he kissed me.

It wasn't rushed. It wasn't demanding. It was slow, deliberate, a question asked with lips instead of words.

My breath caught. My fingers curled into the fabric of his jacket. The room spun—not from the movement, but from the feeling of being seen, wanted, chosen.

When he finally pulled back, his forehead rested against mine.

"Elena," he murmured, "you don't have to forget what he did. But don't let him steal this from you, too."

My chest tightened—not with pain, but with something dangerously close to hope.

I closed my eyes and let myself breathe him in.

Maybe, just maybe, I was ready for this.

The hallway outside the dining room was quiet, the kind of quiet that made every sound feel amplified — the soft click of my heels, the low hum of the ship, the steady rhythm of Julian's breath beside me.

He didn't touch me at first. He didn't have to. His presence alone felt like a hand pressed to the small of my back.

We walked slowly, neither of us speaking, the air between us thick with everything that kiss had awakened. My lips still tingled. My pulse still fluttered. And Julian… he looked like a man trying very, very hard to behave.

Halfway down the corridor, he exhaled sharply.

"Elena," he said, voice low and strained, "you're killing me."

I glanced up at him. "I'm just walking."

"That's the problem."

His hand brushed mine — not an accident, not a mistake. A test. A question. A warning.

I didn't pull away.

He stopped walking. I did too.

The ship rocked gently, and the movement pushed me a fraction closer to him. His breath hitched. His jaw tightened. His eyes dropped to my mouth like he was fighting himself.

"Julian…" I whispered.

He stepped in, slow but deliberate, his body heat wrapping around me like a second skin. His fingers grazed my waist — barely there, but enough to send a shiver racing up my spine.

"You have no idea," he murmured, "how hard it is to keep my hands off you right now."

My breath caught. "Then don't."

His eyes snapped to mine — dark, hungry, startled by how much he wanted that answer.

"Elena," he said, voice rough, "if I touch you the way I want to touch you, I'm not stopping at your hand."

The words hit me like a spark to dry tinder.

I swallowed, my heart pounding. "I didn't ask you to stop."

He closed his eyes for a moment, like he needed the strength not to pin me against the wall. When he opened them again, the restraint was hanging by a thread.

He stepped closer — close enough that my back brushed the wall, close enough that his breath warmed my cheek.

His hand lifted, fingers tracing the line of my jaw, slow and reverent. "You're dangerous," he whispered.

"So are you."

His thumb brushed my lower lip, and my knees nearly buckled.

He leaned in — not kissing me, not yet, just letting his mouth hover over mine, close enough that I could feel the heat of him.

"Elena," he breathed, "tell me to walk away."

I didn't.

Instead, I slid my hand up his chest, feeling the tension coiled beneath his shirt. His breath stuttered. His control cracked.

He kissed me.

Not soft this time. Not careful. A hungry, desperate kiss that tasted like everything we'd been holding back.

My fingers curled into his jacket. His hand slid to my waist, pulling me against him, his body warm and solid and wanting. The hallway spun. The world narrowed to the heat of his mouth and the sound of his breath mixing with mine.

When he finally tore his lips from mine, he rested his forehead against mine, breathing hard.

"We need to stop," he said, though his hands didn't move.

"Why?" I whispered.

"Because if I take one more step with you tonight…" His voice broke into a low, strained growl. "I won't be able to pretend I'm capable of taking things slow."

My pulse throbbed in my throat. "Maybe I don't want slow."

He closed his eyes as if the words physically hit him.

"Elena," he said, voice shaking with restraint, "you've been hurt. You're healing. And I'm not going to be the man who takes advantage of that."

I opened my cabin door, my hand still on his chest. "You're not taking advantage."

He swallowed hard, eyes burning into mine. "Then you're tempting me on purpose."

"Maybe I am."

His hand slid to the doorframe beside my head, caging me in without touching me. His lips brushed my ear — barely, just enough to make my breath catch.

"Goodnight," he whispered, voice thick with desire he refused to act on. "Before I forget what kind of man I'm trying to be."

I stepped inside, trembling.

He stepped back, trembling harder.

The door closed between us, but the heat he left behind stayed with me long after.

Chapter Eight

The sunlight was too bright when I opened my eyes, the kind of bright that made everything from last night feel unreal. For a moment, I lay still, staring at the ceiling, replaying the way Julian had kissed me in the hallway. The way he'd whispered goodnight, like it physically hurt him to walk away.

My body still hummed with the memory.

A knock sounded on my door — soft, controlled, but unmistakably him.

I opened it to find Julian leaning against the frame, hands in his pockets, hair slightly mussed like he'd run his fingers through it one too many times.

"Morning," he said, voice low.

"Morning."

The awkwardness between us was almost comical — two adults pretending they hadn't nearly devoured each other against a wall twelve hours ago.

He cleared his throat. "We docked in Nassau. I thought you'd want to join me for the shore excursion."

I crossed my arms, partly to look composed, partly because my robe suddenly felt too thin. "Is this part of your private tour?"

His eyes flicked down my body before he dragged them back up. "No. This is me asking you on a… morning adventure."

I hesitated — not because I didn't want to go, but because wanting anything felt dangerous.

Julian noticed. "Elena," he said softly, "you don't have to be afraid of wanting something."

I exhaled. "Give me ten minutes."

He smiled — slow, warm, devastating. "Take your time."

The island was a postcard — turquoise water, white sand, palm trees swaying like they were dancing to a rhythm only they could hear. The group excursion led us along a coastal trail, but Julian and I drifted toward the back, walking side by side.

Every time our arms brushed, heat shot through me.

Every time he looked at me, I felt it in places I shouldn't.

Halfway down the trail, we reached a lookout point — a rocky ledge overlooking the ocean. The rest of the group moved ahead, leaving us alone in the shade of a palm tree.

Julian stepped closer, his voice barely above a whisper. "You've been avoiding looking at me all morning."

"I haven't."

"You have." He tilted his head. "Is it because of last night?"

I swallowed. "Maybe."

He stepped closer — close enough that my back brushed the rough bark of the palm tree. His hand lifted, brushing a strand of hair off my shoulder. His fingers lingered on my skin, warm and deliberate.

"Elena," he murmured, "I'm trying very hard to be good."

"Why?"

"Because if I'm not…" His breath hitched. "I'm going to touch you the way I've been thinking about touching you since the moment you opened your door last night."

My pulse throbbed.

"And how is that?" I whispered.

His restraint snapped.

Not violently — but with a slow, devastating surrender.

Julian's hand slid to my waist, fingers curling into the fabric of my dress. His other hand lifted to my jaw, tilting my face up to his. He pressed his body against mine — not grinding, not explicit, just enough to feel the heat of him, the strength of him, the want he'd been holding back.

His thumb stroked the side of my neck, tracing the line where my pulse raced beneath my skin.

"Elena," he said, voice rough, "tell me to stop."

I didn't.

Instead, I placed my hand on his chest — feeling the rapid rise and fall of his breath — and let my fingers slide up to the warm skin at the base of his throat.

His eyes darkened.

He leaned in, his lips brushing the corner of my mouth — not quite a kiss, but close enough to make my knees weaken.

His hand slid up my side, fingertips grazing the curve of my ribcage through the thin fabric of my dress. Not grabbing. Not groping. Just exploring, reverent and hungry.

I gasped softly.

Julian's breath shuddered. "You have no idea what you're doing to me."

"Maybe I do."

He let out a low, helpless sound — half laugh, half groan — and pressed his forehead to mine.

"If I kiss you right now," he whispered, "I'm not stopping at your mouth."

My fingers curled into his shirt. "Maybe I don't want you to stop."

He closed his eyes as if the words physically hit him.

"Elena," he said, voice shaking, "you're going to ruin me."

Before he could kiss me — before I could pull him down to me — the distant sound of the tour guide calling echoed down the trail.

Julian pulled back slowly, breathing hard, his hands still on my waist.

"This isn't over," he said.

I smiled — breathless, flushed, alive.

"I know."

Chapter Nine

The moon hung low over the private cove, turning the waves into molten silver. The rest of the group stayed near the bonfire, but Julian and I drifted farther down the beach, drawn by something magnetic and impossible to ignore.

The moment we were out of sight, the tension snapped like a pulled thread.

Julian caught my wrist gently, turning me toward him. His eyes were dark, hungry, searching my face like he needed permission he already had.

"Elena," he said, voice low and rough, "I can't pretend anymore."

I didn't answer. I didn't need to.

I stepped into him, my chest brushing his, and that was all it took.

He kissed me—deep, urgent, like he'd been starving for the taste of me. His hands slid to my waist, fingers digging in just enough to make my breath catch. I curled my hands into his shirt, pulling him closer, feeling the heat of his body press into mine.

The ocean roared behind us, but all I could hear was the sound of our breathing—fast, uneven, desperate.

Julian's mouth trailed from my lips to my jaw, then lower, brushing the sensitive spot beneath my ear. My knees nearly buckled. "Julian…" I whispered, my fingers sliding up the warm skin at the back of his neck.

He groaned softly, the sound vibrating against my throat. "You're going to undo me."

His hands moved—slow, deliberate—exploring the curve of my hips, the small of my back, the line of my thigh. Not rushing. Not grabbing. Just learning me, mapping me, savoring every inch he touched.

I arched into him, unable to stop myself.

His breath hitched. "Elena… if you keep doing that…"

I didn't stop.

He pressed me gently back into the warm sand, his body hovering over mine, close enough that I could feel every line of him. The heat between us was almost unbearable.

His hand slid up my side, fingertips brushing the edge of my ribs, the underside of my breast through the thin fabric of my dress. The touch was light—barely there—but it sent a shockwave through me.

I gasped, my back arching.

Julian's breath stuttered. "Tell me to stop."

"I won't."

Julian groaned softly, the sound low and helpless. "You're driving me insane."

His forehead dropped to my shoulder, his breath hot against my neck. I felt him tremble, as his hands explored my body with slow, reverent desperation. His fingers brushed the inside of my thigh, and my breath hitched so sharply he froze.

His hand slid higher, his touch firmer now, more certain. My back arched off the sand, my fingers digging into his shoulders as heat pulsed through me.

The waves crept closer, misting our skin, cooling the sweat that glistened along his jaw, his neck, his chest. He kissed me again — slower, deeper, his tongue brushing mine in a way that made my whole body tighten.

His hands moved with purpose now, exploring every curve, every inch of exposed skin, his breath growing heavier, hotter, more ragged.

"Elena," he whispered against my lips, "I want all of you."

My heart stuttered. "Then take me."

He let out a sound — half groan, half prayer — and pressed his forehead to mine, his breath shaking.

"You're going to ruin me," he said, voice raw.

"Maybe I already have."

His hands slid up my thighs, his body pressing me deeper into the sand, his breath hot and uneven as he kissed down my neck, across my collarbone, and lower still. My fingers tangled in his hair, pulling him closer, needing him closer.

My hands slipped beneath his shirt, tracing the hard lines of his stomach and the warmth of his skin. When he slid deep inside me, his movements were hard and fast, stealing my breath. We moaned together as his body shuddered, tightening above mine as he released inside me. I came at the same time, clenching around him, lost in the intensity of the moment.

The world blurred — the stars spinning overhead, the ocean roaring, the heat between us felt like the night itself might catch fire.

Not lust. Not revenge. Something deeper. Something terrifying. Something real.

I was falling for him.

Hard.

And when Julian lifted his head, sweat glistening on his brow, his chest rising and falling against mine, I saw it in his eyes too — the same fear, the same hunger, the same impossible pull.

"Elena," he whispered, voice shaking, "I'm falling in love with you."

Chapter Ten

The first thing I felt was warmth.

Not the sun, not the sand — him. Julian's arm was draped over my waist, his chest pressed against my back, his breath slow and steady against the curve of my neck. The world was quiet except for the soft hiss of the waves and the distant crackle of the dying bonfire.

For a moment, I didn't move.

I just let myself feel it.

The safety. The heat. The impossible tenderness of a man who had held me like I was something precious.

When I finally opened my eyes, the sky was a pale lavender, the first hint of dawn stretching across the horizon. The tide had crept closer in the night, brushing our feet with cool foam. My dress was rumpled, his shirt unbuttoned, our bodies tangled in a way that made my heart twist.

Julian stirred behind me, his hand tightening at my waist as if he sensed I was awake.

"Elena…" His voice was rough with sleep, warm and intimate in a way that made my chest ache. "Are you okay?"

I turned slowly, facing him. His hair was mussed, his jaw shadowed, his eyes soft in a way I hadn't seen before. Vulnerable. Almost uncertain.

"I'm more than okay," I whispered.

Relief washed over his face, followed by something deeper — something that made my pulse skip.

He brushed a thumb across my cheek, slow and gentle. "I meant what I said last night."

My breath caught. "Julian…"

"I'm not taking it back," he murmured. "Not in the daylight. Not ever."

The honesty in his voice hit me harder than the waves. I felt it settle in my chest, warm, terrifying, and real.

Before I could answer, a shout echoed from down the beach — the excursion guide calling for everyone to head back to the fire.

Julian sighed, pressing his forehead to mine for a brief, stolen moment. "We should go."

I nodded, but neither of us moved.

Not yet.

Not while the world was still quiet. Not while the sunrise painted his skin gold. Not while the memory of last night still clung to us like saltwater.

When we finally stood, Julian laced his fingers through mine — not asking, not hesitating, just choosing me.

And for the first time in a long time, I didn't feel broken.

I felt wanted. I felt seen. I felt… hopeful.

The sand was cool beneath our feet as we walked, but my skin felt warm everywhere he had touched me. Every step made the night replay in flashes, the way he'd whispered my name like it meant something, the way he'd held me afterward like he wasn't ready to let me go.

I wasn't ready either.

The bonfire was little more than glowing embers now, a soft orange pulse against the brightening sky. People were stirring, gathering their bags, brushing sand from their clothes. But when Julian and I stepped into view, still holding hands, still wrapped in the quiet intimacy of dawn, a few curious glances flicked our way. Julian didn't seem to notice. Or maybe he didn't care.

His thumb brushed the back of my hand again, a small, grounding gesture that made my heart flutter. It was ridiculous how something so simple could feel so intimate.

"You're quiet," he murmured, leaning closer so only I could hear.

"I'm thinking," I admitted.

"About last night?" I nodded.

He exhaled softly, like he'd been holding his breath. "If you're second-guessing anything."

"I'm not," I said quickly, surprising both of us. "I'm just…trying to understand how something that should terrify me feels so right."

Julian's expression softened. "Good. Because I don't want you regretting anything."

"I don't, "I said, and I meant it. "Not a single thing."

A slow smile tugged at his lips, not the cocky smirk he'd worn on the balcony, not the teasing grin he'd flashed during the excursion. This one was different. Real. Quiet. Almost reverent.

"Then I'm glad," he said.

We reached the boats, and he helped me in, steadying me with both hands at my waist. The touch was innocent, but my breath still hitched. His fingers lingered a second longer than necessary, and when he finally sat beside me, our knees brushed.

The boat rocked gently as it pushed off from the shore, the engine humming beneath us. The others chatted softly, but Julian and I stayed silent, wrapped in our own little world.

The sun crested the horizon, casting a golden path across the water. I watched it shimmer, feeling something inside me shift, something deep and unfamiliar. I wasn't supposed to feel this way. Not so soon. Not after everything I'd been through.

But grief had hollowed me out. Betrayal had cracked me open. And somehow, impossibly, Julian had slipped into the empty spaces and filled them with warmth.

He leaned closer, his shoulder brushing mine. "You're doing that thing again."

"What thing?"

"Thinking too hard."

I let out a breathy laugh. "Maybe I'm allowed to think after a night like that."

He tilted his head, studying me with those dark, steady eyes. "Just don't think yourself out of something good."

My pulse skipped. "Is that what this is?"

His voice dropped, low and certain. "It could be."

The boat hit a small wave, jolting us closer. His hand found mine again, fingers threading through like it was the most natural thing in the world.

And it was.

As the ship grew larger in the distance, gleaming in the morning light, I felt a strange mix of anticipation and fear curl in my stomach. Last night had changed something, not just between us, but inside me.

I wasn't the woman who had boarded this cruise.

I wasn't the woman who had cried in a motel room.

I wasn't the woman who had begged Todd for honesty; he never gave.

I was someone new. Someone braver. Someone who had let herself be held, seen, wanted, and had wanted back.

When the boat finally docked at the ship's platform, Julian stood and offered me his hand. I took it without hesitation.

As he helped me up, he leaned in, his lips brushing the shell of my ear.

"Don't disappear on me today," he murmured.

A shiver ran down my spine. "I wasn't planning to."

"Good," he said, his breath warm against my skin. "Because I'm not done with you yet."

My heart thudded, loud, and certain.

Neither was I.

I wasn't just falling for him.

I was already halfway gone.

Chapter Eleven

His fingers laced through mine like it was the most natural thing in the world.

"Come with me," I said softly.

He didn't ask where. He just followed.

We didn't talk much on the walk back to my cabin. We didn't need to. Every brush of his fingers, every glance he stole when he thought I wasn't looking, said enough.

When the door closed behind us, the quiet wrapped around us like a blanket.

Julian exhaled, running a hand through his hair. "I feel like I'm still on that beach."

"So do I."

He stepped closer, but not to kiss me. Not yet. He just rested his forehead against mine, breathing me in like he needed the moment to settle something inside himself.

I opened the door to my cabin, and we just wanted to be together, lying on the bed together, we curled up, with limbs tangled, the sheets cool against our sun-warmed skin. His arm draped over my waist, my head on his chest, listening to the slow, steady rhythm of his heartbeat. It felt like the safest place in the world.

By the time we ordered breakfast, the sun was high enough to spill gold across the room. Julian insisted on calling.

"Two coffees," he said into the phone. "A fruit plate. And your best pancakes with eggs and sausage."

He hung up and dropped back onto the bed beside me, his hair tousled, his shirt half-buttoned, looking unfairly good for someone who barely slept.

"You like pancakes?" I teased.

"I'm going to love watching you eat pancakes and sausage."

I laughed, and he smiled like the sound meant something to him.

We ate on the bed, sharing bites, stealing glances, brushing knees. It felt intimate in a way last night hadn't — softer, quieter, more dangerous.

Because this wasn't just a desire.

This was a connection.

Julian set his fork down, his expression shifting. "There's something I want to tell you."

My stomach tightened. "Okay."

He leaned back against the headboard, eyes on the ceiling for a moment before he spoke.

"I'm an architect," he said. "I design buildings. Homes. Spaces people live their lives in."

I smiled softly. "That suits you."

"You'd think so." He let out a breath. "But I didn't start out wanting to build things. I started out wanting to escape them."

I frowned. "What do you mean?"

"My dad was a contractor," he said quietly. "He built houses for other people but never stayed in one long enough for it to feel like home. We moved constantly. New town, new school, new everything. I never unpacked fully. Never made friends. Never… rooted."

My chest tightened. "Julian…"

"When I was sixteen, he left. Just… gone. No note. No explanation." He swallowed. "My mom fell apart. I had to grow up fast. Too fast."

I reached for his hand. He let me take it.

"So, I became an architect," he continued. "Because I wanted to build something that lasted. Something solid. Something no one could walk away from."

I squeezed his fingers. "That's not running. That's healing."

He looked at me then — really looked — and something in his eyes softened.

"Your turn," he murmured.

I hesitated. My past wasn't dramatic. It was quieter. But in some ways, more painful.

"I spent years trying to be the woman Todd wanted," I said. "Perfect. Predictable. Easy. I stopped doing things I loved. I stopped asking for what I wanted. I stopped… being myself."

Julian's jaw tightened. "He didn't deserve you."

"I know that now. But I didn't then."

He shifted closer, brushing a thumb across my cheek. "You're not that woman anymore."

"No," I whispered. "I'm not."

He leaned in, his forehead touching mine. "Good. Because I like this version of you. The one who laughs. The one who fights back. The one who knows what she wants."

My breath caught. "And what do you think I want?"

His lips brushed mine — soft, warm, certain.

"Me," he whispered.

And the terrifying part?

He was right.

His lips had barely left mine when he drew in a slow breath, like he was bracing himself.

"There's… more I should tell you," he said.

I shifted, propping myself on an elbow so I could see him better. "Okay."

He rubbed his thumb over my knuckles, thoughtfully. "I haven't exactly been great at relationships."

A small, humorless smile tugged at his mouth.

I've dated," he said. "A few times, seriously. But I always chose women who didn't really want to know me. Not the real me. They liked the version of me that looked good on paper, the architect, the calm one, the guy who could fix anything except himself."

My chest tightened. "Julian…"

"One of them, Maria- she said I was "emotionally unavailable." He huffed out a breath. "She wasn't wrong. I kept everything surface-level. Safe. I never let anyone close enough to see the mess underneath."

He looked at me then, eyes steady, vulnerable in a way that made my heart ache.

"You're the first person I've wanted to tell the truth to."

I swallowed, the weight of that settling warm and heavy in my chest.

Before I could respond, he brushed a strand of hair behind my ear. "What about you? You said Todd wasn't the only thing you walked away from."

I nodded, exhaling slowly. "There's something I didn't tell you last night."

His brows lifted slightly, inviting me to continue.

"I bought a house," I said. "In Florida."

His eyes widened. "You did?"

"Yeah." I laughed softly, shaking my head. "It still feels unreal. It's small, nothing fancy. But it's mine. I bought it right before this trip. I haven't even moved in yet."

Julian's expression shifted, surprise, then admiration, then something deeper.

"That's huge," he said quietly. "That's...brave."

"It felt like reclaiming something," I admitted. "A life I actually chose. A place I can make my own. A place I don't have to shrink to fit into."

He squeezed my hand, his voice low. "I'm proud of you."

The words hit me harder than I expected. Maybe because no one had said them to me in a long time. Maybe because he meant them.

I let out a shaky breath. "I didn't tell many people. I didn't want anyone's opinions. I just wanted…a fresh start."

Julian shifted closer, his forehead brushing mine again. "You deserve that. A place that feels like home. A place that doesn't ask you to be anything but yourself."

His fingers traced slow circles on the back of my hand, grounding, gentle.

“And for what it’s worth,” he murmured, “I think anyone would be lucky to be part of that new beginning.”

I felt my heart stutter, not in fear, but in recognition.

Because for the first time in a long time, I wasn’t afraid of wanting something.

Or someone.

And Julian was looking at me like he felt the same.

Chapter Twelve

The breakfast tray sat abandoned at the foot of the bed, but neither of us seemed to notice it anymore. The room was warm with sunlight, but warmer still with the quiet, familiar closeness that had settled between us — the kind that only comes after two people have already crossed every line, they thought they wouldn't.

Julian leaned back against the headboard, one arm stretched behind him, the other resting on my thigh as it belonged there. Not tentative. Not testing. Just… natural. His thumb traced slow, absent circles against my skin, and every pass sent a soft ripple of heat through me.

We'd already been here — skin to skin, breath tangled, bodies learning each other in the dark. That knowledge hummed between us now, quiet but unmistakable.

"You're thinking again," he murmured, his voice low and warm.

"So are you."

His lips curved. "I always think about you."

"About what?"

He didn't answer immediately. Instead, he let his hand slide a little higher on my thigh — not rushed, but with the easy confidence of a man who already knew the shape of my body, the way I reacted to his touch.

My breath caught, and his eyes darkened just slightly.

"That," he said softly, "is what I think about."

I shifted closer, my knee brushing his hip, my hand resting on his chest. His heartbeat quickened under my palm — not wildly, but enough to tell me he felt it too. Felt us.

"Julian…"

He turned toward me fully, his knee brushing mine, his hand sliding from my thigh to my waist with a slow, deliberate glide that made my pulse stutter. He pulled me gently into his lap, and the movement felt so natural, so familiar, that my body responded before my mind caught up.

His hands settled on my hips, warm and sure. "You have no idea what you do to me."

"I think I do."

He let out a soft, breathless laugh — the kind that came from somewhere deep, somewhere unguarded. "Last night changed everything."

"For me too."

His expression shifted — heat and tenderness tangled together. He brushed his thumb along my jaw, tilting my face up to his.

"Elena," he whispered, "I can't look at you the same way anymore."

"How do you look at me now?"

His lips hovered just above mine, his breath warm against my mouth. "Like someone I've already had my hands on… and still can't get enough of."

Heat curled low in my stomach.

His fingers slid up my back, tracing the path they'd taken the night before — slow, reverent, remembering. My body leaned into his instinctively, recognizing him, craving him.

He kissed me, not rushed, but deep and knowing, the kind of kiss that said we've already been there, and I want to go again. His hands tightened at my waist, pulling me closer, and I felt the familiar warmth of him, the way he responded to me without hesitation.

The tension wasn't new. It was a spark reigniting something that had already burned hot.

He broke the kiss just long enough to rest his forehead against mine, breathing hard.

"Elena," he murmured, "you undo me."

I smiled softly, brushing my fingers along his jaw. "Good."

I unbuttoned his shirt and ran my hands down his chiseled body. It made my heart race and only made me want him more. I climbed off his lap and worked my way down his body. His cock was already hard, straining against his shorts. I freed it and admired how long and thick it was, standing tall and hard just for me.

I looked up at him and saw pure passion and desire on his face as I lowered my mouth onto his hard cock. A soft moan left his lips as I moved up and down, sucking eagerly and savoring every sound of his pleasure. When he was close to releasing, I stopped and climbed back onto his lap, lowering myself down onto him. As he filled me, I moaned, the feeling of him deep inside sending a rush of pure bliss through my entire body.

I wanted this with him, and I knew he wanted it too. I moved up and down on his cock, drawing closer to my climax.

"Cum on my dick, babe," he whispered.

The pure lust in his words made my pussy contract as I released, soaking him. The way I clenched around him, and the warmth of me pushed him over the edge. He couldn't hold back any longer and filled me with his release, making my whole body tremble.

My cheek rested against Julian's shoulder, his arms wrapped around me, our breaths slowly syncing as the world outside the cabin faded into nothing. His skin was warm beneath my palms, his heartbeat steady and strong under my ear.

I whispered that I was falling for him, and I felt his smile before I saw it — soft, real, unguarded.

"Good," he murmured.

We stayed like that, tangled in sheets and each other, until the ship's gentle hum reminded us that afternoon was creeping in. Eventually, Julian shifted just enough to look at me, brushing a thumb along my cheek.

"Come with me today," he said. "The next island… It's special. I want to share it with you."

I nodded, unable to stop the smile that rose to my lips. "I'd like that."

We dressed slowly, not out of hesitation but because every small movement seemed to draw us back to each other, a brush of fingers as we reached for our shoes, a shared smile when he handed me my sunglasses, the way he stood behind me for a moment to fix the strap of my dress that had slipped off my shoulder.

When we finally stepped outside, the sunlight hit us in a warm, bright wave. The ocean stretched out in every direction, glittering like someone had scattered diamonds across the surface. The breeze carried the faint scent of salt and sunscreen, and somewhere in the distance, laughter drifted from the upper deck.

Julian reached for my hand without thinking, or maybe he did think, and that was the point. His fingers threaded through mine, warm and sure, and the simple gesture sent a quiet thrill through me.

"Boat leaves in ten minutes," he said, nodding toward the dock where a small group of passengers was already gathering.

"We should hurry," I said.

"We have time." His thumb brushed the back of my hand, slow and deliberate. "I want to walk with you."

So, we did.

Down the sun-warmed path, past the rows of cabins and the soft hum of morning activity. Every few steps, he glanced at me like he was memorizing something: the way the wind lifted my hair, the way I smiled when he squeezed my hand, the way I looked at him like I wasn't trying to hide anything anymore.

When we reached the boarding ramp, he stopped and turned to face me fully.

"You ready?" he asked.

"For the island?" I teased.

"For all of it," he said quietly.

The breeze lifted the edge of his shirt, sunlight catching in his eyes, and for a moment, the world felt impossibly still.

I squeezed his hand. "Yeah. I'm ready."

He smiled, slow, warm, a little disbelieving, and guided me toward the boat.

Side by side.

Like it was the most natural thing in the world.

Chapter Thirteen

The boat carried us to a small, secluded island — a crescent of white sand and turquoise water framed by lush green cliffs. It felt untouched, like a secret the world had forgotten.

The boat slowed as it neared the shore, and the moment Julian helped me step onto the sand, it felt like we'd crossed into another world. The island was quiet except for the soft rush of waves and the distant call of birds hidden somewhere in the trees.

"Before we swim," Julian said, brushing his thumb across the back of my hand, "I want to show you something."

He led me along a narrow path that curved around a cluster of palm trees. The sand warmed beneath our feet, and the air smelled faintly of hibiscus. A few minutes later, the trail opened into a small clearing where a row of kayaks waited, bright red and yellow against the pale sand.

"You want to kayak?" I asked. His grin was boyish, almost mischievous.

"Only if you're up for it."

I'm up for anything with you."

Something flickered in his eyes at that, something warm, something that made my stomach flutter.

We pushed one of the kayaks into the shallows and climbed in, Julian settling behind me. His knees bracketed my hips, his hands covering mine on the paddle as he guided us forward. The kayak glided easily across the glassy water, each stroke sending ripples shimmering behind us.

"Look to your right," he murmured.

I turned and gasped.

A school of silver fish darted beneath the surface, moving like a single shimmering ribbon. Sunlight caught their scales, turning them into flashes of quicksilver.

"It's beautiful," I whispered.

"So are you," he said softly, and even though I didn't turn around, I felt the sincerity in his voice like a warm hand against my spine.

We paddled farther out, the cliffs rising around us like protective arms. The world felt impossibly still, just the two of us, the kayak, and the endless blue.

After a while, Julian rested his paddle across his lap. "You know, "he said, "I didn't expect this trip to feel like…. more."

"More?" I echoed.

"More than a break. More than a distraction. More than a week away from work." His voice dropped, quieter. "I didn't expect to meet someone who made everything feel different."

My breath caught, but he wasn't finished. "I've had flings," he admitted. "Short things. Safe things. Things that didn't ask anything of me." He paused, the kayak rocking gently beneath us. "But this doesn't feel like that. You don't feel like that."

I turned slightly, enough to see him over my shoulder. His expression was open and unguarded, in a way that made my heart ache.

"I don't want this to be just a vacation thing," he said

The words settled deep inside me, warm and steady.

"I don't either," I said quietly.

His hand slid to my waist, fingers curling there with a kind of reverence. "Good."

We drifted for a while, letting the current carry us, neither of us needing to speak. Eventually, Julian tapped my shoulder.

"Ready to head back?"

"Yeah."

We paddled toward shore, our movements easy, in sync. When the kayak scraped gently against the sand, Julian hopped out first and offered me his hand. I took it, and he pulled me close, and kissed mt temple.

"Come on," he said softly. "Let's go cool off."

He laced his fingers through mine again, leading me toward the water. The ocean stretched out before us, warm and inviting, sunlight dancing across its surface like scattered gold.

We stepped in together, the waves curling around our ankles, then our calves, then our waists. The water lifted us, wrapped around us, drew us closer. And when he finally pulled me into his arms, the rest of the world faded away.

The sun warmed our skin, the breeze carried the scent of salt and flowers, and for the first time in a long time, I felt light.

We splashed in the waves, playfully splashing water at each other and laughing, when he turned and smiled at me and said.

"You're beautiful," he said with so much love and passion.

Heat bloomed in my chest. "Thank you."

"Absolutely."

He swam closer, his hands finding my waist beneath the water. The touch was gentle, but it sent a shiver through me — not from cold, but from the memory of how close we'd been hours earlier.

I slid my arms around his shoulders, the water lifting us, pulling us together. Our bodies floated, pressed chest to chest, the ocean rocking us in a slow, natural rhythm.

Julian brushed his nose against mine. "I could stay like this forever."

I smiled, my fingers tracing the back of his neck. "Me too."

He kissed me then — soft, warm, lingering — the kind of kiss that wasn't about hunger or urgency, but about connection. His hands slid up my back, guiding me closer, the water swirling around us as if it were part of the moment.

When he pulled back, he rested his forehead against mine.

"Elena," he whispered, "I don't want this to be just a vacation thing."

My breath caught. "I don't either."

His arms tightened around me, holding me against him as the waves lapped at our shoulders. The world felt small, quiet, perfect — just the two of us suspended in blue water and sunlight.

"Then let's see where this goes," he said softly. "No fear. No past. Just us."

I nodded, my heart full. "Just us."

And in that moment — wrapped in his arms, the ocean warm around us, the sun painting his skin gold — I knew I wasn't just falling.

I am in love with this man!

Chapter Fourteen

The sun was high by the time we left the water, our skin warm and salty, our fingers still laced together like neither of us had any intention of letting go. The island stretched out before us—white sand, swaying palms, and a quiet that felt like it belonged only to us.

Julian carried the small picnic basket the excursion staff had packed, but he kept glancing at me like I was the real view. Every time our eyes met, something fluttered in my chest—soft, warm, terrifying in the best way.

We found a spot beneath a palm tree, the shade cool and dappled. The ocean glittered just a few feet away, waves rolling in with a lazy rhythm. Julian spread out the blanket, and I sank onto it, pulling my knees to my chest as he settled beside me.

"This is perfect," I murmured.

He smiled, brushing a strand of hair behind my ear. "Not yet."

He reached into the basket, pulling out fruit, sandwiches, sparkling water… and then something else. A small, leather-bound sketchbook.

My breath caught.

"You draw?" I asked softly.

He hesitated—just for a moment—before handing it to me. "I don't show this to many people."

I opened it carefully.

The first few pages were landscapes, buildings, bridges, and cityscapes. Beautiful, precise, full of emotion. But when I turned another page, my breath stilled.

It was me.

Sitting on the deck of the ship, hair blowing in the wind, eyes half-closed like I was listening to something only I could hear. The lines were soft, tender, intimate in a way that made my heart ache.

"Julian…" My voice cracked. "When did you draw this?"

"The first night," he said quietly. "You were alone on the railing. You looked… peaceful. Like you were finally breathing after holding it in for too long."

I traced the sketch with trembling fingers. "It's beautiful."

"You're beautiful," he said simply.

Heat rushed to my cheeks. I closed the sketchbook gently, holding it against my chest.

"Why didn't you tell me?"

He shrugged, a little shy for the first time since I'd met him. "I didn't want to scare you off. And I didn't want you to think I was… I don't know. Obsessed."

I laughed softly. "Julian, you're the least scary man I've ever met."

He raised a brow. "You sure about that?"

I leaned in, brushing my lips against his cheek. "Positive."

He exhaled, relief softening his features. "Good."

We ate slowly, feeding each other pieces of fruit, laughing when juice dripped down our fingers. The breeze rustled the palm leaves above us, and the world felt impossibly gentle.

After a while, Julian lay back on the blanket, pulling me down with him until my head rested on his chest. His fingers traced lazy patterns on my arm, sending warm shivers through me.

"Elena," he murmured, "I need to ask you something."

I lifted my head. "What is it?"

He looked suddenly vulnerable—open in a way that made my heart twist. "Last night… this morning… today… I don't want it to be temporary. I don't want to pretend this is just a cruise thing."

I swallowed hard. "It's not."

His eyes searched mine. "Then what is it?"

I took a breath, feeling the truth rise in my chest like a tide I couldn't hold back.

"I'm in love with you," I said softly. "I don't want to spend a moment without you."

Julian froze—not in shock, but in something deeper. His hand slid to my cheek, his thumb brushing my skin with a tenderness that made my eyes sting.

"Elena," he whispered, "I've been falling for you since the moment I saw you. I just didn't know how to say it."

I leaned down, kissing him—slow, warm, full of everything I felt. His arms wrapped around me, pulling me closer, holding me like he never wanted to let go.

When we finally broke apart, he rested his forehead against mine.

"Stay with me," he murmured. "After the cruise.

My heart swelled. "Yes."

The waves rolled in, the sun warmed our skin, and for the first time in a long time, the future didn't feel scary.

We stayed like that for a while, wrapped up in each other, the world quiet except for the soft rush of the tide and the rustling palms overhead. Eventually, Julian brushed a thumb across my cheek, his expression softening into something almost boyish.

"Come on," he said gently. "There's more I want to show you."

He stood and offered me his hand. I took it without hesitation.

We wandered farther down the shoreline, our footprints trailing behind us in the wet sand. The island curved into a small cove where the water turned and took on an even deeper shade of turquoise. A few colorful fish darted near the rocks, shimmering like living jewels.

Julian pointed toward a narrow path tucked between two palms. "This way."

The trail led us to a lookout point, a small rise overlooking the entire crescent of the island. From up there, the ship looked tiny in the distance, a white speck against the endless blue.

"It's beautiful," I whispered.

He didn't look at the view. He looked at me.

"You are."

I nudged him with my shoulder, trying to hide the way my heart fluttered. "You can't keep saying things like that."

"Why not?"

"Because I might start believing you."

He smiled, slow and warm. "Good."

We sat on a smooth rock, the breeze lifting my hair as Julian leaned back on his hands, eyes half-closed like he was memorizing the moment. I watched him for a long time, the way the sunlight caught in his hair, the relaxed curve of his mouth, the quiet peace in his posture.

He looked…happy.

Really, truly happy.

"Do you ever think about what you want your life to look like?" I asked softly.

He opened his eyes, turning toward me. "I used to think about it all the time. But it always felt like something far away.

Something I wasn't ready for."

"And now?"

He reached for my hand, threading our fingers together. "Now it feels like it's right in front of me."

My breath caught.

We stayed there until the sun dipped lower, painting the sky in soft shades of gold and rose. Eventually, Julian stood and brushed the sand from his shorts.

"We should head back," he said. "They'll start calling for the last boat soon."

I nodded, though a part of me wished we could stay on that island forever, just the two of us, suspended in this perfect, impossible moment.

As we walked back toward the beach, Julian kept my hand in his, swinging it gently between us. The air was warm, the breeze soft, and everything felt…easy.

Halfway down the path, he stopped suddenly.

"Elena."

I turned. "What?"

He stepped closer, cupping my face in both hands. "I meant what I said. I don't want this to end when we get back on that ship."

"It won't," I whispered.

He kissed me, slow, certain, full of promise.

When we reached the shoreline, the boat was already waiting, a few other passengers climbing aboard. Julian helped me into the boat, his hand lingering at my waist, his eyes never leaving mine.

As the boat pulled away from the island, I looked back at the stretch of sand where we'd spent the afternoon, where everything had changed.

Julian slid his arm around my shoulders, pulling me close.

"You okay?" he murmured.

I rested my head against him, feeling the steady beat of his heart beneath my cheek.

"I'm perfect," I said.

And for the first time in a long time, I meant it.

Chapter Fifteen

The boat brought us back to the ship, painting the sky in soft streaks of rose and gold. Julian held my hand the entire way, his thumb brushing slow circles against my skin like he couldn't stop touching me… and I didn't want him to.

When we stepped onto the deck, the evening breeze wrapped around us, warm and gentle. The ship lights flickered on one by one, glowing like stars scattered across polished metal.

Julian leaned close, his lips brushing my temple. "Tonight isn't over."

A shiver ran through me — not from cold, but from the quiet promise in his voice.

When we reached my cabin, I opened the door… and froze.

The room was transformed.

Soft golden lights twinkled around the ceiling. A trail of rose petals led to the balcony. A chilled bottle of champagne sat in a silver bucket beside two glasses. And on the bed, folded neatly, was a card embossed with the cruise line's logo.

I blinked. "Julian… did you do this?"

He looked just as surprised as I was. "No. I swear I didn't."

I picked up the card.

"For the couple who made our staff believe in love again. Enjoy your evening. — The Star of the Seas Crew"

My breath caught. "They… did this for us?"

Julian laughed softly, sliding his arms around my waist from behind. "Guess we weren't as subtle as we thought."

I leaned back into him, feeling his warmth, his steady heartbeat against my spine. "This is beautiful."

"You're beautiful," he murmured, kissing the side of my neck.

We carried the champagne out to the balcony. The ocean stretched endlessly beneath us, dark and shimmering under the moonlight. The ship hummed softly, a gentle reminder that the world was still turning even though it felt like time had stopped.

Julian poured the champagne, handing me a glass. Our fingers brushed — a small touch, but it sent a warm rush through me.

"To us," he said.

"To us," I echoed.

We clinked glasses, the soft chime lost in the sound of the waves.

He watched me for a long moment, his expression shifting — softening, deepening, turning into something that made my heart flutter.

"Elena," he said quietly, "I need to tell you something."

I set my glass down, suddenly breathless. "What is it?"

He took my hands in his, his thumbs brushing my knuckles with a tenderness that made my chest ache.

"I know we haven't known each other long," he began, voice low and steady. "I know this is fast. Maybe too fast. But I can't ignore what I feel."

My heart pounded.

He stepped closer, his forehead resting against mine.

"I don't want this to end when the cruise ends," he whispered. "I don't want to go back to my life and pretend this was just a beautiful week. I want… more. I want everything with you."

My breath trembled. "Julian…"

He cupped my face gently, his eyes shining in the moonlight.

"Elena, I want to spend the rest of my life with you. I know it's crazy. I know it's fast. But I've never been more certain of anything."

Emotion surged through me — warm, overwhelming, real.

I slid my hands up his chest, feeling the steady rise and fall of his breath, the strength beneath my palms.

"I don't think it's crazy," I whispered. "I think it's right. Because I don't want this feeling to end either. I don't want a single day without you."

His breath caught — a soft, broken sound of relief and joy.

"Elena…"

I smiled, tears stinging my eyes. "I'm in love with you. Completely. And I want forever with you, too."

He pulled me into his arms, holding me like he never wanted to let go. The ocean roared below us, the stars shimmered above, and the world felt impossibly perfect.

Julian kissed me — slow, deep, full of everything we hadn't said and everything we had.

Julian didn't let go of me right away. His arms stayed wrapped around my waist, his forehead resting against mine as if he needed a moment to steady himself, or maybe to savor the shift that had just happened between us. I felt it too, that quiet click inside my chest, like something had finally fallen into place.

When he pulled back, his hands slid down my arms, lingering at my elbow before he intertwined our fingers again. "Come here," he murmured.

He guided me to the railing, the two of us standing shoulder to shoulder as the ship cut through the dark water. The moon cast a silver path across the waves, shimmering like a road leading somewhere only we could go.

"I used to think love had to be complicated," Julian said softly. "Hard. Messy. Something you had to fight for every second."

I turned toward him. "And now?"

He looked at me with a tenderness that made my breath catch.

"Now I know it can be simple. It can be this. Just…choosing someone. Every day."

Warmth spread through my chest, slow and steady. "I choose you."

We stood there in silence for a moment, letting the wind wrap around us, letting the truth settle between us like something sacred. The ship lights reflected in his eyes, turning them soft, molten gold. Julian brushed a strand of hair from my face, tucking it gently behind my ear. "You know," he said, voice low, "I didn't expect any of this. I came on this cruise to get away. To breathe. To reset."

"And instead you found me," I teased lightly.

He smiled, the slow, heart-melting smile that made my knees feel unsteady. "I found everything I didn't know I needed."

My throat tightened. "Julian…"

He lifted my hand to his lips, pressing a kiss to my knuckles. "I want to build something with you. Something real. Something lasting."

The sincerity in his voice wrapped around me like a warm embrace. I felt it in my bones, the truth of it, the promise of it.

"I want that too," I said.

He exhaled, a soft sound of relief, and pulled me into his chest. I rested my head against him, listening to the steady rhythm of his heartbeat, feeling the rise and fall of his breath. The world felt impossibly still, like the universe had paused just for us.

And in that moment, wrapped in his arms under the moonlit sky, I knew one thing with absolute certainty:

This wasn't the beginning of the end.

It was the beginning of forever.

Chapter Sixteen

Julian woke before the sun.

Elena was curled against him, her breath soft and warm against his chest, her fingers loosely tangled in the fabric of his shirt. He watched her for a long moment — the rise and fall of her breathing, the peacefulness on her face, the way she instinctively leaned into him even in sleep.

He kissed her forehead.

"I'll be back soon," he whispered.

She didn't stir.

Julian slipped quietly out of the cabin, closing the door behind him with a soft click.

The ship was quiet at this hour; the hallways were washed in soft morning light. Julian walked with purpose, his heart pounding with a mixture of nerves and certainty.

The jewelry boutique had just opened. The attendant looked up with a warm smile.

"Looking for something special?"

Julian nodded. "The most special thing I'll ever buy."

The attendant led him to a case of engagement rings. Diamonds glittered beneath the glass, but Julian's eyes went straight to one — an oval-cut stone set on a band of diamonds that shimmered like moonlight on water.

It was elegant. Timeless. Beautiful.

Just like her.

"That one," he said, voice steady.

When the attendant placed it in his hand, Julian felt something settle inside him — a quiet, powerful certainty.

This was the ring he wanted to see on Elena's finger for the rest of his life.

That evening, Julian led Elena to the top deck just as the sun dipped below the horizon. The crew had outdone themselves — lanterns glowed softly, rose petals lined the walkway, and a small table was set with champagne and candles.

Elena gasped. "Julian… what is all this?"

He didn't answer.

He took her hands, his eyes warm and steady.

"Elena," he said softly, "I know this is fast. I know we haven't had years together. But I also know that what I feel for you… It's real. It's deep. And it's the kind of love people spend their whole lives searching for."

Her breath trembled.

Julian reached into his pocket.

And then he sank to one knee.

"Elena," he whispered, opening the box to reveal the oval-cut diamond that sparkled like a captured star, "will you marry me?"

Tears filled her eyes instantly.

"Yes," she breathed. "Yes, Julian. Of course, yes."

He slipped the ring onto her finger, stood, and pulled her into his arms. Their kiss was soft at first — trembling, emotional — then deepened into something warm and consuming, full of promise and desire.

It felt like it was just them.

Even though we had an audience and everyone was clapping as we kissed under the stars and to the sound of the waves crashing around us, this was the most amazing night, a night we would never forget!

Julian held her for a long moment after she said yes, his forehead pressed to hers, their breaths mingling in the warm night air. The applause around them faded into a soft blur, distant, unimportant, because all he could feel was her. Her heartbeat against his chest. Her fingers were trembling slightly where the clutched his shirt. The way her smile lit up her entire face.

"Elena," he whispered again as if saying her name grounded him. "You've made me the happiest man alive."

She laughed softly, brushing away a tear that had slipped down her cheek. "I can't believe this is real."

"It's real," he murmured, kissing her again.

"All of it."

They stayed on the deck for a few minutes more, letting the moment settle into their bones. The lanterns flickered gently in the breeze, the ocean stretched endlessly around them, and the universe itself had paused to witness their beginning.

When they finally walked back toward the cabin, Julian kept her hand in his, lifting it every few steps to kiss the new ring on her finger. Elena couldn't stop smiling. She didn't even try.

They barely made it through the door before Julian's hands were on her waist, pulling her close, his breath warm against her neck. Elena's fingers slid into his hair, drawing him down into a kiss that was slow at first… then deeper, hungrier, full of the emotion that had been building all day.

He lifted her gently, her legs curling around him as he carried her toward the bed. Their bodies pressed together, warm and familiar, the closeness sending a shiver through her.

"Elena," he murmured against her lips, "I love you."

She cupped his face, her forehead resting against his. "I love you too."

Julian pulled my dress over my head and began kissing me, his lips trailing down my neck until he reached my breasts. He took my nipples into his mouth, sucking and teasing them until I moaned at the incredible sensation. He moved back up and kissed me hard, full of passion and desire, then tossed his shirt onto the floor as I lay back on the bed.

He climbed on top of me and kissed me again as he slid his hard dick into my wet, throbbing pussy. I moaned in anticipation as he began thrusting in and out of me. My back arched against the bed as I climbed closer to my orgasm, and he leaned down, kissing me as he whispered, "Cum for me. Show me how much you love my dick deep inside you."

I let out a loud, uncontrollable moan as I came so intensely it felt like I was flying. As I came down from my high, he was still thrusting hard and fast inside me. I felt his dick grow even stiffer as he reached his own climax. He let out a deep groan as he filled me with his warm release, sending me into another wave of pleasure.

He slid onto the bed beside me, kissed me softly, and said, "Elena, you're amazing, making love to you is so incredible, and I'm so glad I get to do it for the rest of my life."

Julian pulled her against his chest, his hand resting over her heart.

The world outside faded away.

There was only them, the glow of the cabin lights, the sound of the ocean beyond the balcony, the warmth of two people who had found something rare and unexpected.

Julian brushed a strand of hair from her face, his voice barely above a whisper.

"Tonight…I just want to hold you. To remember every second of this."

Elena smiled, her heart swelling. "Then hold me."

And he did.

They curled together beneath the soft sheets, wrapped in each other's arms, sharing quiet kisses and whispered dreams about life ahead, a home, a family, a future built on love and trust and the kind of connection neither of them had ever known before.

Julian rested his hand over her heart, feeling its steady rhythm. "Forever," he murmured.

Elena traced the line of his jaw, her voice soft and sure. "Forever."

And as the ship sailed through the moonlit water, they saw everything waiting just beyond the horizon.

Chapter Seventeen

Elena woke to the soft sound of knocking.

Still wrapped in Julian's arms, she blinked sleepily as he stirred beside her. His voice was rough with morning warmth. "Stay here. I'll get it."

He slipped out of bed, pulling his clothes on as he crossed the room. When he opened the door, he froze.

A small group of cruise staff stood there, beaming, holding trays and gift bags wrapped in shimmering gold paper.

"Good morning, Mr. and Mrs.-to-be," the lead attendant said with a bright smile. "Congratulations on your engagement. The crew wanted to do something special for you."

Elena sat up, pulling the sheet around her, her heart swelling. "Oh my gosh… this is so sweet."

The attendants carried in a beautifully arranged breakfast spread — fresh fruit, pastries, eggs, smoked salmon, chocolate-dipped strawberries, and a bottle of chilled mimosa mix. A small vase of tropical flowers sat in the center, vibrant and fragrant.

Julian looked stunned. "You didn't have to do all this."

"We wanted to," the attendant said warmly. "Your love story has been the talk of the ship. It's been a joy to watch."

Elena felt her cheeks warm as Julian squeezed her hand.

"And these," the attendant added, placing two gift bags on the table, "are from the staff personally."

When the door closed behind them, Elena and Julian exchanged a look — soft, overwhelmed, full of gratitude.

"Open yours," Julian said, sitting beside her on the bed.

Elena pulled out a delicate silver anklet with tiny ocean-themed charms — a dolphin, a seashell, a wave. Her breath caught. "It's beautiful."

He smiled. "It suits you."

"Your turn," she said, handing him his bag.

Inside was a leather-bound travel journal embossed with the ship's emblem and the words "For the Journey Ahead."

Julian ran his fingers over the cover, emotion flickering in his eyes. "Wow. This is… perfect."

They ate breakfast on the balcony, sharing bites, feeding each other strawberries, and laughing. The ocean stretched endlessly before them, shimmering under the morning sun.

Elena rested her head on his shoulder. "I can't believe this is real."

Julian kissed her temple. "It's real. And it's only the beginning."

As they finished breakfast, Elena noticed a small envelope tucked beneath the vase of flowers.

"What's this?" she asked.

Julian opened it, reading aloud:

"A special excursion has been arranged for the happy couple. Meet at the island's marine sanctuary at noon. — With love, The Star of the Seas Crew."

Elena's eyes widened. "I can't wait to see what they have planned."

Julian grinned. "I think we're in for something unforgettable."

She threw her arms around him, laughing. "This ship is spoiling us."

"You deserve to be spoiled," he murmured.

They dressed for the day — Elena in a purple and pink bikini with a flowing white sundress over top that made her look like she belonged in a postcard, Julian in a crisp linen shirt that made her heart flutter all over again.

As they walked hand in hand toward the boat, crew members and the guests they passed offered congratulations, smiles, and warm wishes. It felt like the whole ship was celebrating with them.

Julian squeezed her hand. "Ready for our first adventure as an engaged couple?"

Elena looked up at him, her ring catching the sunlight. "With you? Always."

And together, they stepped onto the boat — hearts full, hands intertwined, ready for the island, and the future they were already building.

The boat skimmed across the turquoise water, warm wind lifting Elena's hair as she leaned into Julian's side. Her engagement ring sparkled in the sunlight, catching flashes of gold and fire with every movement. Julian noticed every glint — and every time, his smile deepened like he still couldn't believe she'd said yes.

When the boat reached the island's dock, the crew greeted them with bright smiles.

"Welcome, Mr. and Mrs.-to-be," one of them said warmly. "Your private excursion is ready."

Elena squeezed Julian's hand. "They're really spoiling us."

Julian kissed her temple. "Good. You deserve it."

The path to the marine sanctuary wound through lush greenery, the air thick with the scent of hibiscus and salt. When they stepped into the clearing, Elena gasped.

A private lagoon stretched before them — crystal-clear water, sunlight dancing across the surface, and two dolphins circling playfully near the edge as if they'd been waiting just for them.

A trainer waved them over. "They're excited to meet you."

Elena's heart fluttered. "Julian… this is incredible."

He watched her with a soft expression. "You're incredible."

They waded into the warm water together, hand in hand. The dolphins swam up immediately, chirping and nudging Elena gently. She laughed — a bright, joyful sound that echoed across the lagoon.

Julian couldn't take his eyes off her.

One dolphin splashed him deliberately, and Elena burst into giggles. "I think they like you."

"I think you're right," he said, brushing a wet strand of hair from her cheek.

They swam with the dolphins, letting them pull them gently through the water, touching their smooth skin, feeding them fish, and laughing like children. At one point, a dolphin nudged Elena toward Julian, pushing her right into his arms.

She wrapped her arms around his neck instinctively.

"Even the dolphins know we belong together," she whispered.

Julian kissed her — slow, warm, tasting of salt and sunshine. "Smart dolphins."

After the swim, the trainer led them down a sandy path to a secluded cove. Elena stopped short when she saw it.

A private beachside lunch had been set up beneath a canopy of palm leaves. A low table draped in blue linen. Cushions are scattered across a woven mat. A chilled bottle of champagne. Plates of fresh fruit, grilled fish, warm bread, and tropical desserts arranged like artwork.

Elena pressed a hand to her chest. "Julian… did you plan this?"

He shook his head, smiling. "The crew did. They said they wanted to give us a day we'd never forget."

She turned to him, eyes shining. "They succeeded."

They settled onto the cushions, toes buried in the warm sand. The ocean stretched endlessly before them, waves rolling in with a soft, rhythmic hush. Julian poured champagne, handing her a glass.

"To us," he said.

"To Forever," she whispered.

They ate slowly, while admiring the beauty of the island and the ocean in front of them. At one point, Julian brushed a crumb from her lip with his thumb, his touch lingering just a moment too long.

"Elena," he said softly, "I've been thinking about something."

She set her glass down, giving him her full attention. "Tell me."

He took her hand, tracing the engagement ring with his thumb. "I want you to move in with me. In Tennessee."

Her breath caught — not in surprise, but in the warm rush of certainty.

"I want that too," she said without hesitation.

Relief washed over his face, followed by a smile that made her heart flip. "And your house in Florida," he continued, "we don't have to give it up. We can keep it. Use it as a vacation home. A place to escape to whenever we want. A place that's ours."

Elena felt tears prick her eyes — the good kind, the overwhelming kind.

"You've really thought about this," she whispered.

"Every detail," he admitted. "Because I want a life with you. Not just a home. A life."

She leaned in, cupping his face in her hands. "Julian… I want all of that. I want mornings with you. Nights with you. A home with you. A future with you."

He kissed her — slow, deep, full of promise.

When they finally pulled apart, he rested his forehead against hers.

"We're really doing this," he murmured.

"We are," she whispered. "And I've never been surer of anything."

After their dolphin swim and beachside lunch, Elena and Julian wandered hand in hand through the colorful streets of Bimini. The island buzzed with life — bright shops, handmade crafts, music drifting from open doorways, the scent of grilled seafood and sweet pastries in the air.

Elena stopped at a small shop selling hand-woven bracelets. "These are beautiful."

Julian picked up a turquoise one and tied it gently around her wrist. "This one matches your eyes."

She blushed. "You're so amazing."

They bought matching bracelets, a carved wooden dolphin, and a small watercolor painting of the island to hang in their home. Every shopkeeper congratulated them when they saw Elena's ring, and Julian couldn't stop smiling.

"You're glowing," she teased.

"That's because I'm with you."

As evening approached, they found a small beachfront restaurant with lanterns hanging from the palm trees and tables set right in the sand. The ocean crashed, shimmering under the fading light.

They ordered grilled lobster, coconut rice, and fresh fruit cocktails. The food was delicious, but Julian barely looked away from Elena.

"You know," he said softly, "I could get used to this."

"Dinner on the beach?"

"Dinner anywhere, as long as you're across from me."

Her heart fluttered. "You're going to make me cry."

He reached across the table, brushing his thumb along her hand. "I'm going to make you happy."

"You already do."

The sky shifted from gold to pink to deep violet as they ate, the lanterns glowing softly around them. It felt like the world had slowed just for them.

After dinner, they kicked off their shoes and walked along the shoreline. The waves lapped at their ankles, warm and gentle. Elena leaned into Julian, her head resting on his shoulder, his arm wrapped securely around her waist.

The sun dipped below the horizon, painting the sky in streaks of orange and purple.

Julian stopped walking and turned her toward him. "Elena," he murmured, brushing a strand of hair from her face, "I can't believe I get to marry you."

She cupped his jaw, her thumb tracing the stubble there. "I can't believe I get to spend my life with you."

He kissed her — slow, deep, full of the kind of love that made her knees weaken. The waves washed over their feet, the breeze lifted her hair, and everything felt incredibly perfect.

When they finally pulled apart, Julian rested his forehead against hers. "Let's go back to the ship."

Her breath caught. "Yes."

They returned to the ship under a sky full of stars, fingers intertwined, hearts racing with anticipation. The moment the cabin door closed behind them, Julian pulled her into his arms, his lips finding hers in a kiss that was warm and hungry all at once.

"Elena," he whispered against her mouth, "I need you."

She slid her hands up his chest, feeling the steady thrum of his heartbeat beneath her palms. "I'm yours, and I want you."

He gently took her hand and led her onto the balcony, then lifted her arms and pulled her dress over her head. It pooled at her feet as he kissed her softly yet intensely, stealing her breath. He untied her top and slid her bottoms down, leaving her standing before him, naked and exposed. He looked her over slowly and murmured, "Your body is stunning."

He shed his clothes without ever taking his eyes off her, desire written across his face. He leaned in and kissed her neck, sending shivers down her spine and making her ache for him. Turning her around, he bent her over a chair on the balcony and took her from behind. She felt his hard cock slide into her wetness as he gripped her hips and pushed deeper, drawing a breathless moan from her lips.

"Harder, babe," she whispered. "I want you to fuck me harder."

He answered by thrusting more forcefully as her pleasure built. Reaching around, he found her clit and rubbed it while driving into her, pushing her over the edge. She cried out, shaking with pure, orgasmic bliss.

As he neared his own climax, she pulled away and said softly, "I want to taste all of you." She wrapped her mouth around him, sucking and teasing until he released, warmth filling her mouth. He looked down at her as she swallowed, his eyes widening in awe.

She licked her lips and smiled. "You taste amazing."

He leaned down and kissed her gently. "I love you he whispered as the waves crashed below and they stood naked on the balcony, holding each other.

Later, they lay together wrapped in one another's arms, bare skin pressed close, the ocean humming softly outside the window. With the night around them and each other's warmth to hold, they drifted off to sleep.

Chapter Eighteen

The next morning, the ship docked at a new island, a place so picturesque it looked like it had been painted into existence. Powder-soft sand-colored buildings dotted the harbor like something out of a dream. The air smelled of salt, hibiscus, and warm sunshine.

Julian laced his fingers through mine as we stepped onto the pier. "Ready for another adventure?"

I smiled, lifting my hand so the sunlight caught the diamond on my finger. "More than ready."

Waiting for us at the end of the dock was a horse-drawn carriage, white, trimmed with soft blue fabric, and pulled by a gentle chestnut mare with a braided mane. The driver, an older Bahamian man with a warm smile, tipped his hat. "Congratulations to you both," he said. "I hear we're celebrating love today."

Julian shot me a playful look. "Word travels fast."

The driver chuckled. "On an island this small? News travels faster than the tide."

We climbed into the carriage, settling onto the cushioned seat as the horse began to trot forward. The wheels rolled smoothly over the cobblestone streets, the rhythmic clop of the hooves blending with the distant sound of waves.

The island unfolded around us, colorful markets, children laughing as they chased each other through the square, women weaving baskets beneath palm trees, and fishermen mending nets along the docks.

Everything felt alive, vibrant, full of stories.

Julian slipped his arms around my shoulders, pulling me close. "I could get used to this."

"Being engaged?" I teased.

"Being yours," he said softly.

My heart fluttered.

The carriage turned down a quieter road lined with blooming bougainvillea. The petals drifted in the breeze like confetti, scattering across the path. The driver glanced back at us.

"There's a lookout point up ahead," he said.

"Perfect spot for pictures."

Julian squeezed my hand. "Perfect."

When the carriage stopped, we stepped out onto a small hill overlooking the ocean. The water stretched endlessly, shifting from turquoise to deep sapphire. A photographer from the cruise, a woman with a bright smile and a camera slung around her neck, waved as we approached.

"You must be the newly engaged couple," she said. "Congratulations! Ready to make some magic?"

Julian looked at me like I was the only thing in the world worth photographing.

"We are ready."

The session began with simple poses, holding hands, standing side by side, smiling at the camera. But soon the photographer encouraged us to move, to laugh, to be ourselves.

"Julian, whisper something in her ear," she said.

He leaned in, his breath warm against my skin. "I'm going to marry you," he murmured.

I laughed, the kind of laugh that came from deep inside, full of joy, disbelief, and love. The photographer captured it instantly.

"Beautiful," she said. "Now hold her like you never want to let go."

Julian wrapped his arms around me from behind, his chin resting on my shoulder. I leaned into him, feeling the steady beat of his heart against my back.

"Perfect," the photographer whispered.

We moved to the edge of the hill, where the wind lifted my hair and the sunlight wrapped around us like a blessing. Julian brushed a strand from my face, his touch gentle, reverent.

"Look at each other," the photographer said.

We did.

And the world fell away.

His eyes were warm, full of promise. Mine reflected everything I felt: love, certainty, the quiet awe of knowing I had found my forever.

The photographer lowered her camera. "I think we got it."

Julian kissed my forehead. "I think we did too."

We walked back to the carriage hand in hand, the island glowing around us, the future stretching wide and bright ahead. As the horse carried us back toward the harbor, Julian rested his hand over mine, his thumb brushing the ring he'd chosen with so much care.

"Elena," he said softly, "I can't wait to marry you."

I learned my head on his shoulder. "I can't wait either."

The carriage rolled on, the gentle sway of the seat rocking us into a peaceful silence. The island breeze carried the scent of coconut and sea salt, and every so often Julian would point out something small, a brightly painted shop, a cluster of wildflowers, a pair of parrots perched on a branch, as if he wanted to memorize every detail of the day.

"Look," he murmured, nodding toward a small group of children playing soccer in a sandy lot. Their laughter echoed through the warm air, carefree and bright.

I leaned into him. "This place feels alive."

"It does," he agreed. "But I think it's because of who I'm here with."

My cheeks warmed. "You're getting good at this whole fiancé thing."

He grinned. I've had a very inspiring subject."

The carriage slowed as we approached a quiet stretch of beach, untouched and shimmering under the afternoon sun. The driver turned slightly in his seat.

"Most people don't come down this way," he said. "Thought you two might like a moment alone."

Julian's hand tightened around mine. "Thank you."

We stepped down from the carriage, our feet sinking into the warm sand. The water here was impossibly clear, the kind of blue that didn't seem real. A few seashells dotted the shoreline, and the only sound was the gentle hush of waves.

Julian slipped his arm around my waist.

"Let's walk."

We wandered slowly, our footprints trailing behind us. Every few steps, he would lift my hand to kiss it or brush his thumb over the ring like he still couldn't believe it was real.

"I keep thinking about last night," he said softly.

I smiled. "Me too."

"Not just the proposal," he added.

"Everything. The way you looked at me. The way you said yes. The way it felt like the world stopped for a second."

I leaned my head on his shoulder. "It did."

He exhaled, a soft, content sound. "I want to remember this day forever."

"We will."

We reached a cluster of rocks where the photographer was waiting again, her camera ready. She waved us over with a bright smile.

"Perfect timing," she said. "The light is gorgeous right now."

Julian helped me climb onto a smooth rock, his hands steady and warm. The photographer positioned us so the sun framed us from behind, turning the air around us golden.

"Hold each other," she instructed.

Julian wrapped his arms around my waist, pulling me close. I rested my hands on his chest, feeling the steady beat of his heart beneath my palms.

"Now look at each other."

We did.

And everything else disappeared.

The photographer snapped phot after photo, us laughing, us holding hands, us forehead-to-forehead with the ocean behind us. At one point,

Julian lifted me off the ground and spun me gently, my laughter echoing across the beach.

"That's it!" the photographer called. "That's the shot!"

When she lowered her camera, she smiled warmly. "You two…you're something special. You can feel it."

Julian kissed my temple. "I feel it every second."

We thanked her and walked back toward the carriage, the sun dripping lower, casting long shadows across the sand. The driver helped us back into our seats, and the horse began the slow journey toward the harbor.

Julian rested his hand on my knee, his thumb brushing slow circles, the same way he had on the boat the night before.

"You know," he said quietly, "I used to think love was supposed to be complicated. Messy. Hard."

"And now?"

He turned to me, his eyes warm and steady. "Now I know it can be simple. It can be this. Just choosing someone. Every day."

My heart swelled. "I choose you."

He lifted my hand and kissed the ring again. "And I choose you."

The carriage rolled on, the island glowing in the fading light, the ocean shimmering beside us like a promise.

And as we approached the ship, our ship, I realized something with absolute certainty:

This wasn't just another day on vacation. It was the beginning of the rest of our lives.

Chapter Nineteen

The ship glided smoothly across the open sea, the horizon stretching endlessly in every direction. It was their final full day on the cruise — a day at sea — and somehow it felt like the perfect pause before everything in their lives changed.

Elena woke first, curled against Julian's chest, listening to the steady rhythm of his breathing. His arm tightened around her instinctively, even in sleep, as if his body already knew she belonged there.

She smiled and pressed a soft kiss to his shoulder.

Julian stirred, eyes opening slowly. "Morning, beautiful."

"Morning, fiancé."

He grinned, pulling her closer. "Say that again."

She laughed. "Fiancé."

He kissed her, slow and warm. "Best word I've ever heard."

They spent the morning wandering the ship hand in hand — sipping iced coffees on the deck, watching the waves shimmer under the sun, stopping to browse the shops one last time. More people congratulated them everywhere they went, and Elena couldn't help but glow every time someone noticed her gorgeous ring.

Julian kept brushing his thumb over it, like he still couldn't believe it was real.

Around midday, they lounged by the pool, sharing a plate of fruit and talking about everything — their future home, their favorite moments of the trip, the life waiting for them beyond the ship.

"Tomorrow," Julian said softly, "we start our real life together."

Elena rested her head on his shoulder. "I can't wait."

As the sun dipped lower, they returned to the cabin to get ready for the ship's elegant farewell evening. Elena slipped into a flowing navy dress that hugged her waist and shimmered when she moved. Julian watched her from the doorway, completely undone.

"You look…" He shook his head, stepping closer. "You look like the woman I dreamed I'd marry someday."

Her breath caught. "And you look like the man I never thought I'd find."

Julian wore a crisp blue suit, the top button undone, his hair slightly tousled in a way that made her heart flutter. He took her hand, lifting it to his lips.

"Ready for our last night on the ship?"

"With you? Always."

The dining room glowed with soft golden light, the ocean visible through the panoramic windows. They were seated at a private table near the window so they could see the sunset, with champagne waiting on ice.

Dinner was perfect — tender steak, fresh seafood, decadent desserts — but Elena barely tasted any of it. She was too busy watching Julian, memorizing the way he looked at her like she was the only person in the world.

Afterward, they walked to the top deck where a live band played beneath strings of twinkling lights. Julian pulled her into his arms, swaying with her as the music drifted across the warm night air.

Her head rested against his chest, his hand warm at the small of her back.

"I could dance with you forever," he murmured.

"You will," she whispered.

He kissed her forehead, then her lips — slow, lingering, full of promise.

Around them, the ocean stretched into darkness, the stars shimmering above like blessings.

Later that night, back in their cabin, they packed their bags together. Elena folded her dresses while Julian tucked souvenirs into the side pockets.

Every so often, he'd stop just to pull her into his arms, kissing her like he couldn't help himself.

"Tomorrow," he said softly, "you come home with me."

She smiled, her heart full. "Home. I like the sound of that."

They zipped the last suitcase closed and sat on the edge of the bed, fingers intertwined, the hum of the ship surrounding them.

"Are you nervous?" Julian asked.

"No," she said honestly. "I'm excited. I'm ready."

He kissed her again — slow, deep, full of the kind of love that made her toes curl.

The Florida sun was warm on Elena's skin as she and Julian stepped off the gangway, fingers intertwined, their suitcases rolling behind them. She felt light — like the world had finally shifted into place.

Julian leaned down, brushing a kiss against her temple. "Ready for Tennessee?"

She smiled. "Absolutely."

But as they reached the end of the terminal, a familiar voice cut through the noise.

"Elena!"

It stopped her in her tracks.

Julian's hand tightened around hers, steady and protective.

Todd stood a few feet away, looking disheveled and desperate — like he hadn't slept, like he'd been waiting there for hours. His eyes locked on their joined hands, then on the ring glittering on her finger.

"Elena," he said again, breathless, "please… I need to talk to you."

Julian glanced at her. "Do you want me to stay?"

She nodded. "Yes."

Todd swallowed hard. "I messed up. I know I did. I shouldn't have let Jalisa come between us. I shouldn't have—" His voice cracked. "I'm done with her. I swear. I still love you, Elena. I want to marry you. We can fix this."

Julian stayed silent, but his presence was solid beside her — a quiet promise that she wasn't facing this alone.

Elena took a slow breath. "Todd… I don't love you anymore."

Todd flinched as if she'd struck him.

"I went on this cruise to find myself," she continued, her voice steady, "but instead… I found the love of my life."

Todd's eyes widened. "Elena—"

She held up her hand, the engagement ring catching the sunlight. "Julian and I are engaged."

Todd stared at the ring, disbelief turning to something hollow and aching. "You barely know him."

"I know how he makes me feel," she said softly. "I know that with him, I'm happier than I've ever been. Happier than I ever was with you."

Todd's face crumpled. "Elena, please—"

"I'm sorry," she whispered. "But I'm not coming back. Not to you and not going back to who I was before."

Julian stepped closer, his hand sliding gently to the small of her back — not possessive, just supportive.

Todd looked at him, then at her, then at the ground. "So that's it."

Elena nodded. "That's it."

For a moment, the world went quiet — just the sound of cars, rolling suitcases, and Todd's shallow breathing.

Then Elena turned toward Julian.

"Let's go home."

Julian lifted their joined hands and pressed a kiss to her knuckles. "With pleasure."

They walked away together, leaving Todd standing alone in the bright Florida sun — watching the woman he once took for granted walk into a future that no longer included him.

Elena didn't look back.

She didn't need to.

She had everything she wanted right beside her.

And as Julian opened the car door for her, smiling like she was his entire world, she knew with absolute certainty:

She had chosen right.

She chose a life with the man of her dreams, and she knew he would never hurt her as Todd did.

Chapter Twenty

The highway stretched out before them, sunlight flickering through the trees as Julian's SUV hummed steadily along the road. Elena curled up in the passenger seat, her legs tucked beneath her, her hand resting in Julian's on the center console.

Every so often, he'd lift her hand to his lips and kiss her knuckles, like he still couldn't believe she was really there — engaged to him, choosing him, building a life with him.

"You doing okay?" he asked softly.

Elena smiled. "I'm perfect."

He glanced at her, eyes warm. "Good. Because I've been imagining this drive for days."

She laughed. "You have?"

"Yeah. You, me, the open road… heading home together. It feels like a dream."

She leaned over and kissed his cheek. "It's real now."

He squeezed her hand. "Everything with you is."

By the time they reached the rolling hills of Tennessee, the sun was dipping low, painting the sky in soft pinks and golds. Julian turned onto a quiet road lined with tall trees, their branches arching overhead like a welcoming canopy.

"This is it," he murmured.

Elena's heart fluttered.

They pulled into the driveway of a beautiful craftsman-style home — warm wood, stone accents, a wraparound porch. It looked like something out of a magazine… but more importantly, it looked like him.

And now, it would be theirs.

Julian came around to open her door, offering his hand. "Welcome home, Elena."

She stepped out, breath catching. "Julian… It's beautiful."

He watched her with quiet pride. "Wait until you see inside."

He led her through the front door into a spacious living room with vaulted ceilings, exposed beams, and a stone fireplace. The space felt warm, full of character — like every piece had been chosen with intention.

"This is where I read," he said, pointing to a cozy armchair by the window.

"This is where I sketch," he added, nodding toward a drafting table tucked into a corner.

"And this," he said, turning to her with a soft smile, "is where I imagined you."

Elena's breath trembled. "Julian…"

He took her hands. "I pictured you here long before I knew you. I just didn't know your name yet."

She wrapped her arms around him, holding him close. "I love it. I love you. I love this life we're starting."

He kissed her sweet lips. "Then it's yours. All of it."

They sat together on the couch, legs tangled, her head on his shoulder as they made the calls to their parents to announce their good news.

Elena called her parents first. Her mother squealed so loudly that Julian laughed, and her father kept saying, "As long as he treats you right," to which Julian leaned over and said loudly, "Sir, I promise I will."

Julian's family was next. His sister cried happy tears. His mother insisted they visit soon. Elena felt her heart swell.

When the calls ended, Julian pulled her into his lap, kissing her softly.

"They already love you," he murmured.

She smiled. "I already love them."

The house was quiet, wrapped in the soft glow of evening. Elena walked slowly through the bedroom, fingertips brushing the edge of the dresser, the smooth wood of the doorframe, the soft fabric of the curtains. Everything felt warm and inviting.

Julian watched her from the doorway, leaning against the frame, his eyes dark with something warm and hungry.

"You look like you're already making this place yours," he murmured.

She turned, her breath catching at the way he looked at her — like she was the only thing in the room worth seeing.

"Maybe I am," she whispered.

He crossed the room in a few slow, deliberate steps, stopping just inches from her. His hand lifted to her cheek, his thumb brushing her skin with a tenderness that made her knees weaken.

"Elena," he said softly, "I've wanted this moment since the second I knew you were coming home with me."

She slid her hands up his chest, feeling the warmth beneath his shirt, the steady thrum of his heartbeat. "I've wanted it too."

His breath hitched — a quiet, unguarded sound that sent a shiver through her.

He dipped his head, kissing her slowly at first, savoring her, learning her all over again. But the kiss deepened quickly, heat curling between them, his hands sliding to her waist, pulling her flush against him.

She gasped softly against his mouth, her fingers curling into the fabric of his shirt.

Julian's lips trailed along her jaw, down the side of her neck, each touch warm and lingering. "You have no idea what you do to me," he whispered against her skin.

Elena's breath trembled. "Show me."

He lifted her effortlessly, her legs wrapping around his waist as he carried her toward the bed. The room felt warmer, the air thicker, charged with the kind of tension that made her pulse race.

He laid her down gently, but the look in his eyes was intense. He craved every inch of her, wanting to make her his and only his forever. He climbed on top of me and unbuttoned my shirt, revealing my hardened nipples, already aching with anticipation. He swirled his tongue around them, sucking eagerly, sending sparks of pleasure through me.

He kissed his way down my stomach until he reached my shorts, pulling them and my panties off before trailing kisses along my hips and over my lips. I could feel myself growing wetter with every second, the anticipation of his mouth on me nearly unbearable. He parted me gently and pressed his tongue against my clit, sending shivers through my entire body. He licked and sucked with urgency, making me moan as my climax built.

"Cum on my tongue, babe," he whispered.

My back arched, fingers digging into the sheets as I obeyed, releasing with a cry and soaking his mouth. He moaned softly. "Mmm, babe, I love the taste of you."

He moved to climb back on top of me, but I rolled him over and straddled him instead. I worked my way down his body and pulled off his shorts, freeing his hard dick, already standing tall for me. I wrapped my hand around the base and licked the head slowly before running my tongue down his shaft. He moaned as I took him into my mouth, sucking and teasing until his body tensed and he groaned, releasing into me.

Breathing hard, he said, "I need you. I want you. I need to feel your pussy wrapped around my dick."

I climbed back onto him and slid him deep inside me, riding him slowly as I kissed his lips. Our pleasure built together until he flipped me onto my back and took control, thrusting harder and deeper. I looked into his eyes and saw nothing but passion and love as we both went over the edge together, crying out as our bodies shuddered in release.

It was overwhelming and intense, leaving me lightheaded. He leaned down, resting his weight on me as he kissed me deeply, stealing my breath. When he finally pulled back, he looked into my eyes and confessed, "I am completely, utterly in love with you."

"I feel the same way, babe," I whispered. "I want and need you every day for the rest of my life."

Later, wrapped in his arms beneath the soft glow of the bedside lamp, Julian pressed a kiss to her shoulder, his breath warm against her skin.

"You're everything," he whispered.

Elena turned in his arms, resting her forehead against his. "And you're my home."

He pulled her closer, their legs tangled, his hand resting over her heart.

"Forever," he murmured.

"Forever," she echoed, her voice soft and certain.

And in the quiet of their new home, with the Tennessee night wrapped around them, they drifted to sleep — bodies warm, hearts full, and a future burning bright between them.

Chapter Twenty-One

Elena woke to the soft Tennessee sunlight warming her skin, and Julian's arm wrapped securely around her waist. His breath brushed her shoulder, slow and steady, and the moment she shifted, he pulled her closer like he'd been waiting for her to wake.

She turned in his arms, smiling. "Good morning."

His eyes opened, warm and sleepy. "Morning, sweetheart."

He kissed her — slow, lingering, the kind of kiss that made her toes curl under the sheets.

"Our first morning home," he murmured.

She brushed her fingers along his jaw. "It feels perfect."

After breakfast, a rumble outside caught Elena's attention. She stepped onto the porch just as a large moving truck pulled into the driveway.

Julian came up behind her, sliding an arm around her waist. "Your things?"

She nodded, heart fluttering. "I arranged for a moving company to bring everything from Florida. I needed to feel at home here."

Julian kissed the side of her head. "I'm glad. This is your home now."

The movers unloaded boxes, artwork, and all the pieces of Elena's old life — pieces she was ready to blend into her new home. Julian helped direct where things should go, carrying boxes inside with ease, occasionally stopping just to kiss her or pull her into a quick hug.

At one point, he paused in the doorway, watching her unwrap a framed photo.

"You're really here," he said softly.

She looked up, smiling. "I'm really here."

They spent the afternoon unpacking — opening boxes, arranging furniture, hanging pictures, and folding clothes into drawers. Elena added soft touches everywhere she went, candles, throw blankets, framed photos, little pieces of her personality that warmed the space instantly.

Julian watched her with quiet awe. "You're making this place feel alive."

She walked over and wrapped her arms around his neck. "We're making it ours."

He kissed her forehead. "Best feeling in the world."

Later, they sat at the kitchen table surrounded by notebooks, laptops, and cups of coffee. Elena opened a fresh journal labeled Wedding Plans.

"So," Julian said, leaning back in his chair, "what kind of wedding do you want?"

She smiled, twirling her pen. "Something intimate. Romantic. Something that feels like us."

He reached across the table, taking her hand. "Then that's exactly what we'll have."

They talked about venues — a vineyard, a garden, maybe even an oceanside ceremony. Elena described her dream dress, and Julian listened as every detail mattered.

At one point, he stood, walked around the table, and pulled her into his lap.

"You planning our wedding is the most beautiful thing I've ever seen," he murmured against her cheek.

As the evening settled in, Julian surprised her.

"Get dressed," he said with a mischievous smile. "Something pretty."

She raised a brow. "Where are we going?"

"You'll see."

She chose a soft, flowing dress that made her feel beautiful. Julian wore a crisp button-down that hugged his chest muscles, and it made my heart skip a beat. He took her hand as they walked out the door, locking the house behind them.

Julian didn't tell her where they were going at first. He just drove, his hand resting on her thigh, thumb brushing slow circles that made her feel warm all over.

They passed rolling hills dotted with barns and white-fenced pastures, the kind of scenery Elena had only ever seen in postcards. The late-afternoon sun cast everything in a soft golden glow, turning the fields into waves of amber.

"Where are we?" she asked, watching a herd of horses grazing near a wooden fence.

"Just outside town," Julian said. "There's a place I want you to see."

He turned down a gravel road lined with tall oak trees. At the end of it sat a historic farmhouse turned café, its wraparound porch glowing with string lights. A hand-painted sign read: Sweet Magnolia Market & Café.

Elena's eyes widened. "This is adorable."

"Wait until you taste their peach cobbler," Julian said, grinning.

Inside, the café smelled like cinnamon, butter, and warm fruit. They shared a slice of cobbler topped with melting vanilla ice cream, sitting at a small table by the window. Elena watched the sun dip behind the hills, feeling something inside her settle in a way she hadn't expected.

Afterward, Julian took her to the local artisan market, a converted barn filled with handmade pottery, candles, quilts, and carved wooden signs. Elena wandered slowly, touching everything, her eyes bright with curiosity.

"Look at this," she said, holding up a ceramic mug painted with wildflowers.

Julian smiled. "If you like it, it's yours."

She blushed. "You don't have to…"

"I want to," he said.

She tucked the mug into her bag, her heart fluttering.

From there, he drove her to Hickory Ridge Overlook, a quiet spot locals used for picnics and stargazing. The view stretched for miles, rolling hills, clusters of trees, and a river winding through the valley like a silver ribbon.

Elena stepped out of the car and inhaled deeply. "It's beautiful."

Julian came up behind her, wrapping his arms around her waist. "This is where I come when I need to think."

She leaned back into him. "And now you're sharing it with me."

Of course I am," he murmured. "You're part of everything now."

They stayed there until the sky turned lavender and the first stars appeared.

Elena rested her head on Julian's shoulder, feeling the quiet peace of the moment settle into her bones.

Eventually, he kissed her temple. "Ready for one more stop?"

She smiled. "There's more?"

"Oh, sweetheart," he said, lacing their fingers together, "there's always more."

He drove them into the heart of town, a charming Tennessee square with twinkling lights strung between lampposts, small shops, and cozy restaurants. Elena pressed her hand to the window, taking it all in.

"It looks like a movie," she whispered.

Julian parked in front of the little bistro with candles glowing in the windows. Inside, they shared wine, warm bread, and a meal that tasted even better because of the way Julian kept looking at her, like she was the only thing in the world worth noticing.

After dinner, they wandered through the square, stopping to peek into shop windows, admire the old brick buildings, and listen to a street musician playing soft guitar near the fountain.

Julian tugged her gently toward the center of the square, beneath a canopy of lights.

"Dance with me," he murmured.

"There's you," he said softly. "That's enough."

He wrapped his arms around her, and she rested her head on his chest as they swayed slowly beneath the lights. His hands were warm at her waist, his breath brushing her hair.

The world felt still. Safe. Right.

"I love this town," she whispered.

Julian smiled against her hair. "I love you everywhere."

He kissed her, slow and deep, full of promise.

And as they walked back to the car, fingers intertwined, Elena knew with absolute certainty:

She wasn't just unpacking boxes. She was unpacking a whole new life, one she was ready to live, love, and grow in with Julian by her side.

Chapter Twenty-Two

The next morning, Elena and Julian sat together on the couch, laptops open, coffee cups steaming between them. Sunlight poured through the windows, warming the hardwood floors of their new home. It felt like the perfect day to take the next step.

Julian nudged her knee with his. "Ready to pick our wedding venue?"

Elena smiled, her heart fluttering. "I still can't believe we're doing this."

He kissed her cheek. "Believe it. You're stuck with me."

She laughed softly, leaning into him. "Good. That's exactly where I want to be."

They scrolled through photos of beaches — white sand, turquoise water, palm trees swaying in the breeze. Elena paused on one image: a secluded stretch of shoreline with a wooden arch draped in soft white fabric, waves rolling gently behind it.

"That one," she whispered.

Julian leaned closer, his arm sliding around her shoulders. "You love it?"

"I feel it," she said. "It looks like us."

He studied her face, not the screen. "Then that's where we'll get married."

She turned to him, eyes shining. "Just like that?"

"Just like that," he said softly. "If it makes you happy, it's perfect."

Her heart swelled. "Julian… you make everything feel easy."

He kissed her forehead. "Because loving you is easy." I can't believe we will be getting married on a beautiful beach in Hawaii.

They drove to Julian's mom's house first, a cozy home with a swing on the front porch and a garden full of wildflowers. The kind of place that felt lived-in and loved. Before they even reached the steps, the front door swung open.

"Elena!" his mother exclaimed, hurrying toward her with open arms. She pulled her into a warm, motherly hug that smelled like lavender and fresh bread. "We've heard so much about you."

His sister appeared next, practically bouncing with excitement. The moment she spotted the ring, she squealed loud enough to startle the birds in the trees. "Oh my gosh, it's gorgeous! Let me see!"

Elena laughed, holding out her hand as Julian's sister examined the ring like it were a rare gem. "Julian did good," she said, winking.

Elena felt instantly embraced, not just welcomed, but wanted. Julian watched her with quiet pride, his hand resting on her back, his eyes soft with affection.

Inside, the house was warm and inviting. Family photos lined the walls—birthdays, holidays, vacations. Julian as a little boy with messy curls. Julian as a teenager holding a trophy. Julian at Christmas, wearing a ridiculous sweater.

Elena found herself smiling at every picture.

His mother insisted on making coffee and bringing out a plate of homemade cookies.

His sister and mom told stories about Julian's childhood, the time he tried to build a treehouse and fell out of the tree, the time he got lost at the county fair because he was too busy staring at the architecture of the booths, the time he declared at age ten that he would "build houses that never fall down."

Julian groaned, burying his face in his hands. "Mom, please."

Elena laughed, her heart swelling. She loved seeing this side of him, the boy he used to be, the man he had become.

Later, when they stepped outside for air, Julian slipped his arms around her from behind, resting his chin on her shoulder.

"They adore you," he whispered.

She smiled, leaning back into him. "I adore them too."

He kissed her cheek. "Ready for round two?"

"Let's do it."

Her mother opened the door before they even knocked, tears already welling in her eyes. She pulled Elena into a tight hug, holding her like she never wanted to let go.

"You look so happy," her mother whispered, brushing a hand through her hair.

"I am," Elena said softly, her voice warm with truth.

Her father stepped forward next. He shook Julian's hand with a firm, protective grip, the kind that said *I'm watching you.* His eyes searched Julian's face, weighing him, measuring him, making sure this man was worthy of his daughter.

"Take care of her," he said quietly, but with unmistakable seriousness.

"I will," Julian promised. "Always."

Her father nodded, but he didn't let go of Julian's hand right away. His voice thickened with emotion. "We never want to see her hurt like she was before. Not ever again. She went through enough because of Todd. She deserves peace. She deserves joy."

Julian's expression softened, sincerity shining through. "I know what she's been through," he said gently. "And I swear to you, I'll spend my life making sure she never feels that kind of pain again."

Her mother wiped her eyes, stepping closer. "She's our girl," she whispered.

"Seeing her broken like that…it nearly broke us too. But seeing her now? She smiled through her tears. "She's glowing. And that's because of you."

Julian slipped an arm around Elena's waist, pulling her close. "She's glowing because she's finally getting the love she deserves."

Her father's expression softened, the tension easing from his shoulders. "Well," he said, clearing his throat, "come inside. Dinner's almost ready."

Inside, the house smelled like home, garlic bread, roasted chicken, and her mother's famous mashed potatoes. They sat around the table sharing stories, laughter filling the room like it had always been meant to be there.

Julian told her parents about the proposal, about the island, about the ring. Her mother cried again. Her father pretended not to, but Elena saw him swipe at his eyes when he thought no one was looking.

At one point, Julian reached under the table and took Elena's hand, giving it a gentle squeeze. She looked at him, and he smiled, soft, full of love, full of certainty.

Their families blended effortlessly, like two puzzle pieces that had been waiting for each other.

And as Elena looked around the table, at her parents laughing with Julian, at the warmth in the room, at the way everything felt so right, she felt something settle inside her.

And for the first time in a long time, Elena felt completely loved and completely home.

Later that night, back in their Tennessee home, Elena stood in the kitchen, staring at the beach venue photo on her phone.

Julian came up behind her, wrapping his arms around her waist, his chin resting on her shoulder.

"You okay?" he murmured.

She nodded, but her voice trembled slightly. "I never thought I'd be planning another wedding this soon."

Julian turned her gently to face him, his hands warm on her hips. "If it's too fast…"

"No," she said quickly, placing her hands on his chest. "It's not that. It's just…I didn't expect any of this. I didn't expect *you*."

His expression softened. "Elena…"

She took a breath, her eyes shining. "But I'm glad I found you. You've completely changed my life. You've made me so happy. Happier than I've ever been."

Julian cupped her face, his thumb brushing her cheek. "You've changed mine too."

She smiled, tears gathering at the corners of her eyes. "I can't wait to marry you."

His breath caught, a soft emotional sound, and he pulled her into a deep, tender kiss. The kind that said everything words couldn't.

When they finally pulled apart, he rested his forehead against hers.

"I can't wait to call you my wife," he whispered.

"And I can't wait to call you my husband."

Chapter Twenty-Three
2 Months Later Their Wedding Day!

The warm ocean breeze lifted the edge of Elena's veil as she stood at the top of the sandy aisle, her arm wrapped tightly around her father's. The soft lace of her gown shimmered in the sunlight — delicate, romantic, and absolutely perfect for a beach wedding. Her heart fluttered, not with nerves, but with a deep, steady certainty.

This was the moment she had been waiting for.

Her father squeezed her hand gently. "You look beautiful, sweetheart."

Elena smiled, eyes already stinging with emotion. "Thank you, Dad."

Then she looked up.

And everything else disappeared.

Julian stood barefoot in the sand, wearing tan pants, a crisp white shirt, and a matching tan vest that hugged his broad shoulders and chiseled chest. The breeze blew his hair; the sun warmed his skin — but none of that compared to the expression on his face.

Tears filled his eyes the moment he saw her.

Real, unguarded tears.

He lifted a hand to his mouth, overwhelmed, his chest rising sharply as if he'd forgotten how to breathe. His eyes never left hers — not for a second.

Elena felt her own tears spill over. This was the man she was about to marry. The man she had found by accident. The man who had become her everything.

Her father squeezed her arm. "He's looking at you like you hung the moon."

"I feel like the luckiest woman in the world," she whispered.

The music began — soft, romantic, carried by the wind — and Elena took her first step. Guests rose to their feet, but she barely noticed them. All she saw was Julian, waiting for her with a heart full of love.

Every step brought her closer to the life she had dreamed of but never thought she'd find.

The aisle was lined with white lanterns and seashells, the petals beneath her feet forming a soft trail of blush and ivory. The ocean sparkled behind Julian, waves rolling in like a blessing.

When she reached him, Julian lifted her veil with trembling hands. "Elena… you're breathtaking."

She smiled through her tears. "So are you."

Her father placed her hand in Julian's, giving a small nod before stepping back. And suddenly, it was just the two of them — standing in the sand, surrounded by the ocean, ready to promise forever.

The pastor smiled warmly. "Julian and Elena have chosen to write their own vows."

Julian went first.

Julian's Vows

He took her hands, his voice thick with emotion. "Elena… I never expected to meet you. Not on a cruise. Not when I wasn't looking. But the moment I saw you, on the balcony, something inside me shifted. You brought light into my life; you warmed my heart. You are everything I didn't know I needed. You've healed parts of me I didn't realize were broken. I promise to love you with everything I am, every day of my life."

Elena's breath trembled, tears slipping down her cheeks.

Then it was her turn.

Elena's Vows

"Julian… I went on that cruise to find myself. I didn't expect to find you. I didn't expect to fall in love so quickly, so deeply, so completely. But you showed me what real love feels like — safe, steady, passionate, and kind. You've changed my life in every way. I promise to love you fiercely, to stand by you, and to choose you every single day."

Julian wiped her tears with his thumb, his own falling freely.

The pastor's voice carried over the waves. "By the power vested in me, I now pronounce you husband and wife."

Julian let out a soft, emotional laugh — half disbelief, half joy.

"You may kiss your bride."

He cupped her face and kissed her with a tenderness that made the world blur. The guests cheered, the ocean roared behind them, and Elena felt her heart burst with happiness.

When they finally pulled apart, Julian rested his forehead against hers.

"Mrs. Foster," he whispered, voice full of awe. "You're my wife."

"And you're my husband," she breathed.

The pastor lifted his voice. "Ladies and gentlemen, it is my honor to introduce, for the very first time… Mr. and Mrs. Julian Foster!"

The crowd erupted in applause as Julian lifted Elena's hand triumphantly, pulling her into another kiss — this one full of joy, passion, and the beginning of forever.

Chapter Twenty-Four

The sun dipped low over the ocean, turning the sky into a watercolor of gold and rose as Elena and Julian walked hand in hand into their beachside reception. Lanterns swayed gently in the breeze, casting warm light across the tables draped in soft white and teal linens. The sound of waves blended with soft music, creating a dreamlike atmosphere.

Julian leaned down, brushing his lips against her ear. "My wife," he whispered, savoring the words.

Elena's heart fluttered. "My husband."

Guests cheered as they stepped onto the sand, glowing with happiness.

The music shifted, and Julian took her hand, guiding her to the center of the dance floor. He pulled her close, his hand warm at her waist, his forehead resting gently against hers.

"You're everything I ever wanted," he murmured.

Elena smiled, tears gathering in her eyes. "And you're everything I never knew I needed."

They swayed slowly, barefoot in the sand, the world fading until it was just the two of them — husband and wife, wrapped in each other's arms.

Julian's sister raised her glass first.

"To the couple who proved that love can find you anywhere — even in the middle of the ocean."

Laughter rippled through the crowd.

Elena's father stood next, his voice thick with emotion. "I've never seen my daughter this happy. Julian, thank you for giving her the love she always deserved."

Julian squeezed Elena's hand, his eyes shining.

Her mother added softly, "And thank you, Elena, for showing us that second chances can be the most beautiful ones."

Their cake was simple and elegant — white frosting, seashell accents, and a topper shaped like two dolphins intertwined. Julian fed Elena a bite, and she laughed when he dabbed a bit of frosting on her nose. She returned the favor, and he kissed the sweetness from her mouth, making the guests cheer.

Later, as the reception wound down and the stars shimmered above, Elena tugged Julian's hand.

"Walk with me," she whispered.

They wandered down the beach, away from the music and laughter, until they stood alone beneath the moonlight. The waves rolled gently at their feet.

Julian brushed a strand of hair from her face. "What's on your mind, sweetheart?"

Elena took a breath, her heart pounding with excitement. "I've been waiting for the right moment to tell you something."

His expression softened instantly. "You can tell me anything."

Her eyes filled with happy tears. "Julian… I'm pregnant."

For a heartbeat, he froze — breath caught, eyes wide — and then emotion washed over him like a wave.

"Elena…" His voice broke. "Are you serious?"

She nodded, tears slipping down her cheeks. "Yes. We're going to have a baby."

Julian pulled her into his arms, lifting her off the sand as he spun her around, laughing and crying all at once.

"Oh my God," he whispered against her neck. "You've made me the happiest man alive. I love you. I love our baby. I love our life."

She held him tightly, her heart overflowing. "I wanted to tell you today… the day we married and became a family."

Julian kissed her — deep, emotional, full of awe. "This is the best wedding gift I could ever imagine."

Their beachfront suite glowed softly with candlelight when they entered, the sound of waves drifting through the open balcony doors. Julian closed the door behind them and turned to Elena with a look that made her breath catch — warm, hungry, reverent.

"My wife," he murmured, stepping closer. "You're my wife."

"And you're my husband," she whispered, her voice trembling with anticipation.

He cupped her face, kissing her slowly at first — savoring her — then deeper, fuller, as if he couldn't get close enough. His hands slid to her waist, pulling her against him, their bodies fitting together with a familiar, electric heat.

Elena's fingers curled into his shirt, her breath catching as he kissed along her jaw, her neck, each touch sending warmth through her entire body.

Elena turned so Julian could unzip her wedding dress. It slid to the floor at her feet as she turned back to him, wearing white, lacy, see-through lingerie. Julian's mouth fell open at the sight of her.

"Oh my God, you are so sexy and gorgeous," he said, desire burning in his eyes, as if he couldn't get enough of her.

He unbuttoned his vest and shirt and tossed them onto the floor. His chiseled body, sculpted abs, and defined happy trail made her breath catch. She dropped to her knees and unfastened his pants, looking up into his eyes as she did. Julian grabbed her hands, pulled her up, and pressed her back against the wall. He lifted her onto his thick, throbbing cock, her legs wrapping around his waist.

He moved her up and down against him as she wrapped her arms around his neck, kissing him deeply, tasting every part of his mouth. Slowly, her climax built deep inside her. She clutched him tighter, moaning into his ear as her body shuddered in pure ecstasy and she came, releasing against him.

She whispered, "I love having your dick deep inside me. Cum for me, babe. I want to feel your warmth inside me. Fuck me harder and show me how much you love that I'm your wife."

He let out a deep groan and thrust harder, his cock growing even firmer inside her as he neared his release. He pulled her close and groaned again as he spilled himself deep inside her.

He laid her down on the bed and looked into her eyes. "Having you as my wife is a dream come true. I'm going to make love to you all night to show you how much I need and want you."

Tears filled her eyes as she kissed him deeply, never wanting to let go.

His shaft brushed against her lips as they kissed, his body already ready for her again. "I just can't get enough of you," he murmured. "Even your kiss makes me hard."

"Then show me again how much you want me," she replied.

He slid back inside her, hard and throbbing. Her back arched off the bed as he filled her, and she felt complete, utterly in love with Julian. She couldn't take her eyes off him as he thrust harder and faster. She screamed and moaned as another orgasm tore through her, and he pulled her in close, groaning deeply as he came again inside her wet, trembling body.

He lay beside her afterward, whispering in her ear, "I love you, my beautiful wife." He placed his hand on her belly and added softly, "And I love our little baby that we created."

The night didn't end there. They made love again and again, wanting and needing each other until exhaustion finally claimed them. Much later, they collapsed into the bed, wrapped in each other's arms beneath the soft glow of moonlight. Julian pressed his hand to her stomach.

"Our baby," he whispered, awe in every word.

Elena smiled, resting her hand over his. "Our future."

He kissed her forehead, her lips, her fingertips. "I love you more than I ever thought possible."

"And I love you," she whispered, drifting to sleep against his chest.

Their wedding night was a night they would never forget, and it was the beginning of a new chapter, a new family, a new forever.

Chapter Twenty-Five

Three weeks after the wedding, Elena lay on the exam table, her hand wrapped tightly in Julian's. The room was dim, quiet except for the soft hum of the ultrasound machine warming up. The faint scent of antiseptic mixed with lavender from the diffuser in the corner creates a strangely calming atmosphere.

Julian sat beside her, his thumb brushing slow circles over her knuckles, a habit he'd developed whenever he was nervous or overwhelmed. Today, he was both.

The technician rolled her stool closer, smiling warmly. "Alright, you two. Ready to see your little one?"

Julian let out a shaky breath. "More than ready."

Elena squeezed his hand. "Here we go."

The gel was cold on her skin, and the technician moved the wand gently across her lower belly. The screen flickered, static at first…then something began to take shape.

A tiny curve. A small flutter. A little bean-shaped silhouette.

Julian froze.

His breath caught in his throat. His eyes filled instantly.

"That's…that's our baby," He whispered, voice breaking.

The technician nodded, her smile softening. "And there's the heartbeat."

She tapped a button, and suddenly the room filled with rapid, rhythmic thumping, strong, steady, impossibly fast.

Julian pressed his free hand over his mouth, tears spilling down his cheeks. He leaned forward, staring at the screen like it was the most miraculous thing he had ever seen.

"Oh my God," he whispered. "Elena…that's our baby."

Elena wiped her own tears, her heart swelling so much it almost hurt. "Yes," she whispered, "and we made it with so much unconditional love."

Julian kissed her forehead, her cheek, her hand, unable to contain the emotion pouring out of him. His shoulders shook with quiet sobs, but his smile never faded.

"I love you," he murmured against her skin.

"And I love this little one more than I ever thought I could."

He rested his forehead against hers as the heartbeat continued to echo around them, sealing the moment into their hearts forever.

The technician printed out several photos and handed them over. Julian held them like they were made of glass, delicate, precious, and priceless.

Elena woke up to the soft glow of sunlight filtering through the curtains and the gentle weight of Julian's arm draped over her wrist. He was already awake, watching her with a tenderness that made her heart flutter.

"How long have you been staring at me?" she asked sleepily.

He smiled, brushing a strand of hair from her face. "Long enough to realize I'm the luckiest man alive."

She laughed softly, leaning into his touch.

"You're going to be such a good dad."

Julian's eyes softened even more, something she didn't think was possible. "I want to be. I want to give this baby everything I never had. Everything I did have, and more."

He rested his hand over her stomach, still flat, still unchanged, but now holding the most precious secret in the world.

"Hi, little one," he whispered. "It's Daddy."

Elena's breath caught. She had never heard him sound so gentle, so full of awe.

Over the next few weeks, their lives fell into a new rhythm, prenatal vitamins, and Elena's sudden cravings for the strangest things.

One night, she nudged Julian awake at 2 am.

"I need…pickles," she whispered dramatically.

Julian blinked, half-asleep. "Pickles?"

"And chocolate. "

He sat up immediately. "Both? Together?"

She nodded seriously. "Yes."

He didn't question it. He just kissed her forehead, grabbed his keys, and said, "I'll be right back."

When he returned twenty minutes later with three jars of pickles and four different kinds of chocolate, Elena burst into tears.

"You're so good to me," she sniffed.

Julian laughed softly, pulling her into his arms. "I'd drive across the country if you needed me to."

That evening, their home buzzed with the warm chaos of family. Elena's parents and Julian's mom arrived carrying dishes, desserts, and the kind of excited energy that always filled the house when everyone was together. Julian's sister came bouncing through the door with a bottle of sparkling cider, insisting it was "for a toast, obviously."

Elena and Julian exchanged a glance, the kind that said *this is it.*

They waited until everyone had settled in the living room. The fireplace crackled softly, casting a warm glow across the room. Elena sat beside Julian on the couch, her hand tucked into his, her heart pounding with anticipation.

Julian cleared his throat, standing up with the ultrasound photos hidden behind his back. "We, uh… have something we want to share with all of you."

Instantly, all conversation stopped.

His mother leaned forward. "What is it, sweetheart?"

Julian looked at Elena, his eyes soft, full of emotion. She nodded.

He lifted the ultrasound photos.

"We are having a baby."

For a heartbeat, the room was silent. Then everything happened at once.

Elena's mother gasped, her hands flying to her mouth as tears spilled down her cheeks. "Oh my goodness…oh my goodness!" She rushed forward, pulling Elena into a tight hug. "My baby is having a baby."

Julian's mother let out a joyful cry, hugging her husband before rushing to Elena. "Let me see! Let me see the pictures!" She held the ultrasound like it was the most precious thing she'd ever touched. "Look at that little peanut!"

Julian's sister squealed so loudly that the neighbors probably heard. "I'm going to be an aunt! Oh my gosh, oh my gosh!" She hugged Julian, then Elena, then Julian again. "I'm buying baby clothes tomorrow. I don't care if we don't know the gender yet."

Everyone talked at once, congratulations, questions, excitement, and happy tears. The room filled with warmth, laughter, and the kind of joy that wrapped around Elena like a blanket.

Julian slipped an arm around her waist, pulling her close as their families celebrated around them.

"This baby is already so loved," she whispered.

Julian kissed her temple. "Just like its mom."

Her mother hugged her again, whispering, "You're going to be an amazing mother."

Julian's mother added, "And Julian…he's going to be a wonderful father."

Elena looked around the room, at the people who had raised them, supported them, and loved them, and felt something settle deep inside her.

A week later, they invited their closest friends over for a casual dinner. Elena wore a soft sweater that hugged her just enough to show the slightest hint of a bump.

Halfway through dessert, Julian stood and cleared his throat.

"We have something to share, "he said, his voice warm with pride.

Elena stood beside him, slipping her hand into his.

"We're having a baby," she said.

The room erupted in cheers, hugs, and happy tears. Their friends surrounded them, touching Elena's belly gently, congratulating Julian, offering advice, and telling stories.

Julian kept his arms around her the entire time, his thumb brushing her shoulder, his smile never fading.

This wasn't just a pregnancy announcement.

It was the beginning of a new chapter. A new generation. A new kind of love.

And as Julian intertwined their fingers, smiling at her with that soft, heart-melting look, Elena knew:

Their baby was coming into a world overflowing with love, and into a family that already felt complete.

Later that night, as they curled up in bed watching a movie before bed, Elena suddenly gasped.

Julian sat up straight. "What? What's wrong?"

She grabbed his hand and pressed it to her stomach. "I think…I think the baby just moved."

They waited.

A moment later…a tiny flutter.

Julian's entire face lit up. "Oh my God. Oh my God, Elena, I felt that."

He laughed, a breathless, joyful sound, and kissed her over and over, unable to contain himself.

"That's our baby," he whispered against her skin. "Our little miracle."

Chapter Twenty-Six

The backyard was filled with soft pastel decorations, a table of treats, and a crowd of smiling faces. Elena stood beside Julian, her hand resting on her growing belly, her heart fluttering with excitement.

Julian kissed her temple. "Ready to find out who's in there?"

She nodded, breath trembling. "Let's do it."

Together, they pulled the ribbon on the confetti cannon.

A burst of pink exploded into the air, swirling around them like rose-colored snow.

Gasps. Cheers. Laughter.

Julian froze for a heartbeat — then his face broke into the widest, most emotional smile she had ever seen.

"A girl," he whispered, voice cracking. "We're having a little girl."

Elena laughed through her tears as he wrapped his arms around her, lifting her off the ground.

"Our daughter he murmured against her neck. "Elena… we're going to have a daughter."

Julian kissed her — soft, emotional, full of awe. "And she's going to have the best mom in the world."

One quiet evening, Elena lay curled on the couch, her head resting in Julian's lap. He stroked her hair gently, humming under his breath.

Suddenly, she gasped.

Julian sat up straighter. "Elena? What is it?"

She grabbed his hand and placed it on her belly. "Just wait."

A moment passed.

Then — a tiny flutter beneath his palm.

Julian's breath caught. His eyes widened, filling instantly with tears.

"That… that was her," he whispered. "She kicked."

Elena smiled, her own eyes shining. "She's saying hello."

Julian leaned down, pressing a trembling kiss to her stomach. "Hi, baby girl. Daddy's right here."

His voice cracked with emotion.

Elena stroked his hair gently. "She knows."

Julian rested his cheek against her belly, holding her close. "I'll love you both forever."

The baby shower was warm, joyful, and full of love. Soft pink decorations filled the room, tiny dresses hung on a clothesline, and a table overflowed with gifts — blankets, toys, books, and tiny little shoes.

Julian stayed by Elena's side the entire time, one hand always resting protectively on her back or belly.

Her mother hugged her tightly. "You're glowing, sweetheart."

Julian's mother added, "This little girl is already so blessed."

Julian kissed Elena's temple. "Because she has the best mom."

Elena leaned into him, her heart full. "And the best dad."

They opened gifts, shared stories, and celebrated the little life growing inside her. It was a day wrapped in warmth and hope.

Later that night, after the guests had gone and the house had grown quiet, Elena stood in the nursery doorway, one hand resting on her belly. The soft glow of the night-light illuminated the tiny crib, the pastel blankets, and the stuffed animals waiting patiently.

Julian came up behind her, placing his hands on her shoulders.

"You okay?" he murmured.

She nodded. "Just thinking about how much our lives have changed."

Julian turned her gently, brushing a thumb along her cheek. "Changed for the better."

She leaned into his touch. "You make everything feel safe."

"And you make everything feel like home," he whispered.

He kissed her — slow, warm, lingering — the kind of kiss that made her whole body soften against him. His hands slid to her hips, pulling her closer, their bodies fitting together with a familiar, electric heat.

Elena's breath trembled. "Julian…"

He rested his forehead against hers. "I love you more and more every day."

She traced the line of his jaw, her voice soft and full of longing. "Show me."

He lifted her gently, carrying her toward their bedroom as she wrapped her arms around his neck. Their kisses deepened, full of emotion and desire, their movements slow and intimate — not rushed, not frantic, but full of connection.

They held each other close, exploring each other with tenderness and heat, their breaths mingling, their hearts beating in sync. Every touch felt meaningful, every kiss full of devotion. It was passion woven with love, desire wrapped in safety, the kind of intimacy that made Elena feel cherished in every way.

Later that night, after the pink confetti had settled and the last guests had gone home, Elena and Julian sat together on the back porch, wrapped in a soft blanket. The sky above them was clear, dotted with stars that shimmered like tiny diamonds.

Julian rested his hand on her belly, his thumb brushing gently back and forth. "A daughter," he said softly, almost in awe. "I still can't believe it."

Elena leaned her head on his shoulder. "I always wondered what it would feel like to say those words."

"And now?" he asked.

She smiled. "It feels perfect."

Julian let out a quiet laugh, breathless and emotional. "I keep imagining her. Little curls. Big eyes. Running around this yard. Calling me Daddy."

His voice cracked, and Elena's heart melted.

"You're going to be wrapped around her little finger," she teased gently.

"I already am," he admitted without hesitation. "The second that pink confetti went up…I swear, Elena, I felt my whole world shift."

She turned toward him, cupping his cheek. "You're going to be the best girl dad."

Julian's eyes softened. "And you're going to be the most incredible girl mom. She's going to look at you the way I do, like you're the most amazing woman in the world."

Elena blinked back tears. "She's going to have so much love."

Julian nodded, his hand spreading protectively over her belly. "More than she'll ever know."

They sat there for a long time, wrapped in each other and the quiet night, imagining tiny dresses, bedtime stories, scraped knees, first days of school, and a little girl with both of their hearts in her hands.

Julian kissed her forehead. "We're really doing this."

"We are," Elena whispered. "And she's already our whole world."

"I love you," he whispered. "Both of you."

Elena smiled, kissing his chest. "We love you too."

And as they drifted off to sleep, tangled together, Elena felt completely at peace, loved, desired, protected, and ready for everything their future would hold.

Chapter Twenty-Seven

The weeks after the baby shower passed in a blur of excitement, planning, and quiet moments that made Elena fall even more in love with Julian, and with the little girl growing inside her.

Every morning, Julian woke up with his hand on her belly, whispering good morning to their daughter before he even opened his eyes. Every night, he fell asleep with his cheek resting against her stomach, as if listening to her dreams.

Their home was changing. Their hearts were changing. Everything was becoming more real.

One evening, they sat on the living room floor surrounded by baby name books, sticky notes, and a notebook labeled *Baby Girl Foster*.

Julian tapped his pen against the page.

"Okay, sweetheart. We need to pick a name before she gets here and names herself."

Elena laughed. "She'd probably choose something like Princess Sparkle."

"I'd still call her that," Julian said without hesitation.

They went through dozens of names, some sweet, some classic, some that made them laugh so hard they cried.

But nothing felt right.

Not until Elena looked up at him, her eyes soft. "What about Juliana?"

Julian froze.

His breath caught. His eyes softened instantly. His voice dropped to a whisper.

"After me?"

Elena nodded. "She's your first daughter.

And you're the best man I've ever known. I want her to carry your name…your strength…. your heart."

Julian blinked rapidly, emotion flooding his face. He reached for her hand, lifting it to his lips.

"Elena," he whispered, "that's the most beautiful thing anyone has ever given me."

"So…Juliana Foster?" she asked softly.

He nodded, tears shining in his eyes. "Our little Juliana."

He leaned forward, pressing a kiss to her belly. "Hi, baby girl. Daddy loves your name."

Elena felt her heart swell. It was perfect. She was perfect.

Two months later, they met with a photographer at a quiet field just outside town, tall grass swaying on the breeze, golden sunlight spilling across the landscape like honey.

Elena wore a flowing blush-pink dress that hugged her bump beautifully. Her hair fell in soft waves, and Julian couldn't stop staring at her.

"You look like a goddess," he murmured, kissing her shoulder.

"And you look like a man who's about to cry again," she teased.

He laughed, wiping his eyes. "I can't help it. You're carrying our daughter."

The photographer guided them gently.

"Hold her belly…yes, just like that."

"Julian, whisper something to her."

He leaned in, his lips brushing Elena's ear.

"I can't wait to meet you, baby girl."

Elena's breath trembled.

"Now kiss her forehead."

He did, slow, tender, full of love.

"Perfect," the photographer said softly.

"You two are magic."

They took photos in the field, by an old wooden fence, and beneath a blooming dogwood tree. At one point, Julian knelt and kissed Elena's belly, whispering, "Daddy's here," and Elena felt Juliana kick in response.

"She knows your voice," Elena said, tears filling her eyes.

Julian pressed his forehead to her bump. "And I'll spend my life making sure she always feels safe."

Later that night, they lay in bed, the room dim and peaceful. Julian wrapped his arms around her from behind, his hands resting on her belly.

"She's going to be here soon." He whispered.

"I know," Elena said softly. "Are you ready?"

Julian kissed her neck, slow and warm.

"I've never been more ready for anything."

She turned in his arms, pressing her forehead to his. "You're going to be an amazing dad."

"And you're going to be the most incredible mom," he whispered.

He rested his hand over her belly again.

"Goodnight, Juliana. Daddy loves you."

Elena smiled, tears slipping down her cheeks. "Goodnight, baby girl."

They fell asleep tangled together, hearts full, dreaming of the little girl who would soon change their world forever.

The nursery was nearly finished, with soft pink walls, a white crib, a rocking chair Julian had refinished himself, and tiny pink outfits hanging neatly in the closet.

Julian stood in the doorway on the evening, arms crossed, eyes soft with pride.

"This room feels like her already," he said.

Elena walked over, slipping her arms around his waist. "It feels like our future."

He kissed her cheek. "I can't wait to hold her."

They spent the next few days organizing drawers, folding blankets, and placing stuffed animals around the room. Julian installed shelves, hung framed prints, and even assembled a tiny bookshelf filled with children's stories.

Late one night, Elena found him sitting in the rocking chair, holding a small pink onesie in his hands.

"Julian?" she asked gently.

He looked up, eyes shining. "I just…. I can't believe we get to do this. I can't believe she's ours."

Elena walked over and sat on his lap, guiding his hand to her belly. "She's already so loved."

He kissed her shoulder. "And she always will be."

Chapter Twenty-Eight

The morning their daughter decided to enter the world began softly —
a pale sunrise stretching across the Tennessee sky, the house quiet except
for the gentle hum of anticipation that had been building for months.

Elena woke with a sudden, unmistakable feeling. "Julian," she
whispered, nudging him gently. "I think it's time."

He shot upright instantly, eyes wide, hair tousled, heart already racing.
"Time… time?" he repeated, breathless.

She nodded, smiling through the nerves. "Time."

Julian kissed her forehead, his hands trembling as he helped her up.
"Okay. Okay. We've got this. I've got you."

And he did — every step of the way.

Hours later, Elena lay in a hospital bed, gripping Julian's hand as
another contraction rolled through her. He stayed right beside her, brushing
her hair back, whispering encouragement, kissing her knuckles between
breaths.

"You're doing amazing," he murmured. "I'm right here. I'm not going
anywhere."

When the moment finally came, the room filled with the sound of a
newborn's cry — strong, beautiful, perfect.

Julian's breath caught. Elena burst into tears.

The nurse placed a tiny, pink-cheeked baby girl onto her chest.

"Hello, Julia," Elena whispered, her voice trembling with awe.

Julian leaned over them, tears streaming freely. "She's… she's
perfect," he said, his voice breaking. "Elena, look at her. She's ours."

He kissed Elena's forehead, then Julia's tiny head, overwhelmed by the love flooding through him.

In that moment, the world felt completely full — of hope, of joy, of everything they never expected but now couldn't imagine living without.

Later, when the nurses had stepped out and the room was quiet, Julian sat in a chair beside the bed, cradling Julia in his arms. She was wrapped in a soft pink blanket, her tiny fingers curled around his thumb.

Julian stared at her like she was the most miraculous thing he had ever seen.

"Hi, baby girl," he whispered. "I'm your daddy."

Elena watched him, her heart swelling. She had fallen in love with Julian once on a cruise… Then again, when he asked her to marry him… And now, watching him hold their daughter, she fell in love all over again.

"You're a natural," she said softly.

Julian looked up, eyes shining. "I've never loved anything like this; it's a love I can't describe."

He leaned over, kissing Elena gently. "Thank you for giving me her. Thank you for giving me you, I couldn't imagine my life without you two."

This is the happiest I have ever been in my life, sitting here watching my husband holding our daughter, I am finally completely and utterly happy!

Epilogue

Months later, their home was filled with the soft sounds of baby giggles, lullabies, and the quiet rhythm of a life built on love.

Juliana's nursery glowed with warm light. Her crib was filled with soft blankets and stuffed animals, each one a gift from someone who already adored her. Her parents' hearts were fuller than they ever imagined possible.

The rocking chair creaked softly as Elena swayed, humming a tune she didn't even realize she'd memorized until motherhood made it second nature.

Julian stood in the doorway, shoulder resting against the frame, watching them with a smile that held every emotion he'd ever felt for them, awe, gratitude, love so deep it softened him in ways he never expected.

"You two are my whole world," he said quietly.

Elena looked up, her eyes warm and tired in the most beautiful way. "We found each other in the most unexpected way."

Julian crossed the room, each step slow, reverent. He wrapped his arms around her from behind, resting his chin on her shoulder as he looked down at their daughter, tiny fingers curled around the edge of Elena's shirt, her breath soft and even.

"And it turned into the most beautiful life." He murmured.

Elena leaned into him, letting his warmth settle around her. "I never thought I'd get a second chance at love."

Julian kissed her cheek, lingering there.

"You didn't just get a second chance. You got the right one."

She smiled, tears gathering in her eyes, not from sadness, but from the overwhelming fullness of everything they'd built. "We found love on a cruise…and it brought us here."

Julian pressed a soft kiss to her temple.

"To Forever," he whispered.

Elena rested her head against him. "To forever," she echoed.

Juliana stirred slightly, her tiny hand brushing against Julian's. He froze, then smiled when her fingers curled around his thumb.

"She knows you're here," Elena whispered.

"She always does," he said softly.

They stood like that for a long moment, husband, wife, and their precious daughter, wrapped in the quiet glow of the nursery, the world outside fading into something distant and unimportant.

Elena looked around the room, taking in the soft pink walls, the framed photos from their wedding, and the seashell mobile Julian had made by hand. "It's funny," she said. "I used to think love had to be perfect. Predictable. Safe."

Julian brushed his thumb along her arm.

"And now?"

"Now I know it just has to be real."

He kissed the top of her head. "Real is all I ever wanted."

Juliana let out a tiny sigh, her lips parting in the faintest smile, and Elena felt her heart swell all over again.

"This is our forever," she whispered.

Julian tightened his arms around her. "And it's only the beginning."

Because their story wasn't just about love, it was about unexpected love. Healing love. Forever love.

A love that found them when they least expected it…And stayed for a lifetime.

One Year Later

The backyard looked different now, fuller, brighter, lived in. Toys dotted the grass, a tiny pair of pink sandals lay forgotten near the porch steps, and the wind chimes Elena hung last spring sang softly in the warm afternoon breeze.

Juliana toddled across the patio, her chubby legs wobbling with determination as she clutched her favorite stuffed dolphin. Every few steps, she glanced back to make sure her parents were watching.

They always were.

Julian leaned against the porch railing, arms crossed, a proud smile tugging at his lips. "Look at her go," he said, shaking his head in disbelief. "Wasn't she just a newborn yesterday?"

Elena laughed, brushing a strand of hair behind her ear. "I know. I blinked, and suddenly she's walking."

"Walking," Julian echoed, "and bossing us around."

As if on cue, Juliana squealed and pointed at a butterfly drifting lazily above the flower bed. "Dada!" she declared triumphantly, as though she'd discovered something monumental.

Julian scooped her up, spinning her gently until she giggled. "Yes, baby girl, that's a butterfly."

Elena watched them, her heart swelling the way it always did when she saw Julian with their daughter. A year ago, everything had felt new and overwhelming: sleepless nights, tiny cries, learning how to be parents together. But now, their home felt like the rhythm they'd created with love, patience, and a thousand small moments.

Julian carried Juliana over to Elena. "She wants her mama," he said, though Juliana was already reaching for her.

Elena took her, breathing in the sweet scent of baby shampoo and sunshine. "Hi, my love," she whispered.

Juliana patted Elena's cheeks, then rested her head on her shoulder, content and safe.

Julian stepped closer, wrapping an arm around both of them. His hand slid instinctively to Elena's belly, a gentle, protective touch that had become second nature these past few months. "You know," he murmured, "I still can't believe this is our life."

Elena's free hand covered his, her fingers curling around his warm and steady. "Me neither."

His thumb brushed the curve of her stomach, where the twins shifted softly beneath her skin. "Two boys," he said quietly, awe threading through his voice. "I still can't wrap my head around it."

She smiled, leaning into him. "They're going to adore you."

"They already do," he said, pressing a kiss to her temple. "Every time I talk to them, they start kicking like they're trying to get my attention."

Elena laughed. "That's because they know your voice."

He looked at her then, really looked, with that same expression he'd worn the first time she told him she was pregnant again. A mix of wonder, gratitude, and a love so deep it softened every line of his face.

"You made everything I ever wanted feel possible," he said.

She looked up at him, her eyes warm. "You gave me a life I didn't even know I could have."

They stood there for a moment, the four of them now, wrapped in the golden glow of later afternoon, the world quiet except for the distant hum of cicadas and Juliana's breathing.

"Let's take a picture," Julian said suddenly. "I want to remember this day."

Elena smiled. "Every day with you three is worth remembering."

He set the camera on the porch rail, set the timer, and hurried back to them. As the shutter clicked, Juliana lifted her dolphin into the air, Elena laughed, and Julian rested his hand over her belly, his other arm wrapped around his girls.

Later, when they looked at the photo, they saw exactly what their year had become:

A family. A home. A love that had grown stronger with every sunrise.

Elena rested her head on Julian's shoulder as they watched Juliana toddle around again.

"We did good," she whispered.

Julian kissed the top of her head. "We did amazing."

Juliana toddled toward the garden again, determined to chase the butterfly that had long since disappeared. Elena and Julian watched her go, her tiny legs pumping, her curls bouncing with each enthusiastic step.

"She's fearless," Julian said softly.

Elena smiled. "She gets that from you."

He slipped his hand into hers, their fingers interlacing easily. "She gets her stubbornness from you."

"Excuse me?" Elena laughed, nudging him with her shoulder.

Julian grinned, leaning down to kiss her cheek. "It's one of my favorite things about you."

A warm breeze drifted through the yard, rustling the leaves of the oak tree and carrying the faint scent of the jasmine Elena planted when Juliana was born. The wind chimes tinkled again, soft, melodic, like a lullaby floating through the air.

Elena rested a hand on her belly, feeling a gentle nudge from one of the twins. "They're active today."

They're excited," Julian said. "They know we're out here together."

She rolled her eyes playfully. "You think everything they do is about you."

"Of course it is," he said, feigning seriousness. "I'm their favorite already."

Elena laughed, shaking her head. "You're impossible."

"And you love me anyway."

"I do," she said quietly, the truth of it settling warm and steady in her chest.

Juliana suddenly plopped down in the grass, giggling as she picked a handful of clovers. She held them up proudly. "Mama! Flowahs!"

Elena walked over and knelt beside her, accepting the slightly crushed bouquet.

"They're beautiful, sweetheart. Thank you."

Juliana beamed, then leaned forward to press a sloppy kiss to Elena's cheek before toddling off again.

Julian watched them with a look that made Elena's heart squeeze, soft, reverent, full of love that had only grown deeper with time.

"You're incredible with her," he said

"She makes it easy."

He stepped behind her, wrapping his arms around her waist, his hands settling over her belly again. "You make it easy."

They stood like that for a long moment, the world slowing around them, Julian's laughter drifting through the yard, the twins shifting gently beneath Elena's hands, the sun dipping lower and painting everything in warm amber light.

"Next year," Julian murmured, there will be three little ones running around out here."

Elena exhaled a soft, breathy laugh.

"Chaos."

"Beautiful chaos," he corrected.

She leaned back against him, letting his warmth settle around her. "I can't wait."

Julian kissed the top of her head, lingering there. "Me either."

The sky deepened into shades of rose and gold, the first stars beginning to peek through. Juliana toddled back toward them, arms outstretched, her dolphin plushy dragging behind her.

Elena scooped her up, pressing a kiss to her forehead. Julian wrapped his arms around both of them again, his hand finding her belly.

And in that quiet, glowing moment, surrounded by the life they'd built together, Elena felt it all over again, the certainty, the gratitude, and the love that kept expanding right alongside their family.

Their story wasn't just continuing.
It was blooming and growing.
Becoming something even more beautiful than she'd ever imagined.
Like waves rolling toward the shore, steady and endless.

Five Years Later

The ship looked exactly the same. White hull gleaming in the sun, flags fluttering in the breeze, the familiar hum of the engines beneath the boarding ramp, but everything felt different now. Maybe because Elena wasn't stepping onto it alone this time.

She had a hand wrapped around Juliana's, who was now six and full of opinions, confidence, and questions. And on her other side, Julian carried one of their twin boys while the other clung to his leg, determined to walk "all by myself."

"Mommy, is this *really* where you and Daddy met?" Juliana asked, her eyes wide as she took in the massive ship towering above them.

"It is," Elena said, smiling. "Right on this very same ship."

Julian shot her a look over the twins' heads, the kind of look that still made her heart flip, even after all these years.

"Best detour I ever took," he said.

"Best mistake," she teased.

"Best fate," he corrected, leaning in to kiss her cheek.

The twins, Mason and Marcus, immediately groaned in unison.

"Ewwww," Mason said.

"Stop kissing!" Marcus added, covering his eyes dramatically.

Juliana rolled her eyes like a seasoned older sister. "They're married; you dummies. They're supposed to kiss."

Julian laughed, shifting Marcus higher on his hip. "Come on, crew. Let's get checked in before these two rebel against us."

They made their way up the ramp, the boys bouncing with excitement, Juliana skipping ahead but always circling back to grab Elena's hand. The moment they stepped onto the deck, a warm breeze swept over them, carrying the scent of saltwater and sunscreen, the same scent that had wrapped around Elena the day she met Julian.

"Déjà vu?" he murmured, brushing his fingers against hers.

"More like a full-circle moment," she said.

They found their cabin, bigger than the one Elena had stayed in years ago, but with the same soft lighting and ocean-view balcony. The twins immediately launched themselves onto the bed, giggling, while Juliana pressed her face to the balcony window.

"Can we go explore?" she asked, bouncing on her toes.

"In a minute," Elena said. "Let's get settled in first."

Julian set down the luggage and wrapped his arms around her from behind, resting his chin on her shoulder. "You, okay?"

She nodded, leaning back into him. "Just…. remembering."

He kissed her temple. "Me too."

The boys were already arguing about who got which bunk, Juliana was narrating the entire layout of the room like a tour guide, and the ship's horn sounded in the distance, loud, familiar, and thrilling.

"Alright," Julian said, clapping his hands.

"Who wants ice cream?"

Three small voices shouted "ME!" at the same time.

They headed out together, weaving through the hallways, the twins holding hands so they wouldn't get lost, Juliana skipping ahead but always looking back to make sure her family was behind her.

When they reached the upper deck, the upper deck, the ocean stretched endlessly around them, blue and bright and full of promise.

Elena thought to herself that if we hadn't met on this cruise, then their children, these three little lives, wouldn't exist if not for that one night, that one spark, that one unexpected connection on our balconies.

"Thank you," she whispered.

"For what?" he asked.

"For that first night. For choosing me. For choosing this."

Julian slid his hand into hers and squeezed gently. "I'd choose you a thousand times."

Juliana tugged on Elena's dress. "Mommy, Daddy, look!"

She pointed toward the horizon where dolphins leapt in and out of the waves, their sleek bodies catching the sunlight. The twins squealed, pressing their faces to the glass railing. Juliana leaned against the railing, her eyes shining.

Elena felt Julian's arm wrap around her waist, pulling her close.

"Looks like the universe is giving us a welcome-back show, he murmured.

She smiled, resting her head on his shoulder. "Feels like it."

The kids laughed, the dolphins danced, as the ship moved through the waves, slowly and steadily carrying forward.

Back to where it all started.

The first evening on the ship felt like stepping into a memory wrapped in something entirely new. The dining room glowed with soft golden light, the ocean visible through the wide windows as the sun dipped toward the horizon.

Juliana marched ahead like she owned the place, her braid bouncing behind her. The twins trailed close behind, each holding one of Julian's hands, chattering nonstop about the dolphins they'd seen earlier.

"Mommy, can I get the chocolate lava cake and the strawberry ice cream?" Juliana asked as soon as they sat down.

Elena raised an eyebrow. "You can pick one."

Juliana sighed dramatically. "Fine. I'll think about it."

Marcus immediately pointed at the breadbasket. "I want that."

Mason pointed at the exact same thing. "No, I want that."

Julian laughed, handing each boy a roll.

"Crisis averted."

Dinner was loud, messy, and perfect.

Juliana told the waiter all about how her parents met on this ship (*"They fell in love right here; did you know that?"*). The twins dropped their napkins at least four times each. Julian kept sneaking glances at Elena across the table, the kind that made her heart flutter even after all these years.

When dessert arrived, Juliana finally chose the chocolate lava cake, the twins shared a bowl of vanilla ice cream, and Elena leaned back in her chair, watching her family with full, quiet joy.

"This was a good idea," she said softly.

Julian reached for her hand under the table. "Best one I've had since the last time I stepped onto this ship."

The kids were exhausted by the time they made it back to the cabin. After a whirlwind of baths, pajamas, and three different bedtime stories, the room finally fell quiet. Juliana curled up with her dolphin plushy, the twins snuggled together in their bunk, and within minutes, all three were asleep.

Elena stepped out onto the balcony, the night warm and breezy, the ocean stretching endlessly beneath the moonlight. The ship hummed softly, a familiar sound that tugged at her heart.

Julian joined her a moment later, sliding the balcony door shut behind him. "They're out," he said, brushing his hand off.

"Completely gone."

She smiled. "I'm not surprised. They ran all over this ship."

He stepped behind her, wrapping his arms around her waist, his chin resting on her shoulder. "You, okay?"

"More than okay," she murmured. Being back here…it feels like everything came full circle."

Julian turned her gently to face him. The moonlight caught in his eyes, softening them, deepening them. "I was thinking the same thing.'"

His hand slid down her hips, warm and familiar. "You know," he said quietly, "the last time we were on a balcony on this ship…I was falling for you."

Elena's breath caught. "And now?"

He brushed a thumb along her jaw, slow and reverent. "Now I'm falling. Every day."

She leaned into him, her hands resting on his chest, feeling the steady beat beneath her palms. The air between them shifted, warm, charged, intimate. He kissed her softly at first, then deeper, the kind of kiss that carried years of love, laughter, and late-night whispers.

The ocean breeze wrapped around them, the moonlight painting silver across their skins. Julian's forehead rested against hers, her voice low and full of emotion.

"I love you," he whispered.

"I love you too," she breathed.

He kissed her again, slow, lingering, full of promise, and the world faded until there was nothing but the two of them, the balcony, and the quiet rhythm of the sea. They stayed wrapped in each other a little longer, as the ship slipped deeper into the night, the stars bright above them, the ocean endless below.

Julian brushed his lips along her neck and murmured, "Do you want round two on a balcony…like we did years ago?"

"Of course I do," I breathed, already aching for him.

I turned and kissed him deeply, pouring every want and need into him. I felt his body respond against mine, hardening with desire, and without a word, I sank to my knees. I freed him from his shorts and took him deep into my mouth, loving the way he groaned as I sucked and licked him, slow and deliberate.

"I love watching you suck my dick," he whispered. "It's so sexy."

I didn't stop until he finally gave in, releasing with a deep groan that sent heat flooding through me, leaving me even wetter than before.

"Your turn," I teased. "Have a seat."

I settled onto the patio chair as he pulled my panties down and gently pushed my thighs apart. His mouth kisses around my lips, unhurried, teasing, before his tongue and fingers slide into my warmth. The sensation stole my breath. When he focused on my clit, licking and sucking just right, my back arched, and a loud moan escaped me as I came undone against his mouth.

I turned and knelt on the chair, gripping the back as he slid into me, thick and hard. A moan spilled from my lips as he thrust deep and steady, building me higher and higher until I cried out, my body trembling as another orgasm tore through me.

We switched places, and he sat back while I climbed onto him, rolling my hips as I grinned fast and hard on him. He kissed and sucked on my nipples, sending shivers racing through me as I rocked harder, coming close to the edge. When he was close, I leaned in and kissed him deeply, full of passion and need, until we both went over the edge together, moaning and shaking in each other's arms.

"That was amazing," Julian said, breathless.

"Sex with you is always amazing." I laughed softly, "That is why we have three kids; we can't keep our hands…or our mouths off each other."

As we sat together and watched the waves, holding each other, Julian murmured, "Do you remember the first time that we stood on a balcony on this ship?" "Just you and me…and the ocean."

Elena smiled, her fingers curling into his shirt as she pulled him closer. "How could I forget? "That was the moment we fell in love."

The years fell away in an instant, the first spark, the first kiss, the first night they'd let themselves fall. And now, sitting on the same ship with the moonlight shimmering across the waves, it felt like time had folded in on itself, bringing every version of them together in one perfect moment.

As they sat wrapped in each other's arms beneath the glow of the stars, Elena rested her head against his chest, listening to the steady beat of his heart.

"Five years," she whispered. "And somehow it still feels like the beginning."

Julian kissed the top of her head. "That's because with you… every day is."

She smiled, her eyes drifting to the horizon where the moonlight danced across the waves. The same waves that had carried her toward heartbreak, toward healing, toward him. Toward the life she never knew she deserved.

Inside the cabin, their children slept soundly. Out here, the ocean whispered its endless song.

Elena laced her fingers through Julian's and held on.

"Funny," she said softly. "I thought my story ended the day I boarded this ship alone."

Julian squeezed her hand. "Turns out, it was just the prologue."

The ship cut through the water, steady and sure, carrying them forward, a family, a love, a life built from a single unexpected moment on a balcony years ago.

Elena closed her eyes, letting the breeze kiss her skin, letting the memories settle around her like warm sunlight.

Some stories are written in ink. Some are written in choices.

Hers was written in something far more powerful, the waves!!

www.ingramcontent.com/pod-product-compliance
Lightning Source LLC
Chambersburg PA
CBHW071337150726
47997CB00002B/758